A LITERARY ADVENTURE
IN AN EMOTIONAL UNDERWORLD.

"Carson McCullers tells her tale with simplicity, insight,
and a rare gift of phrase. She makes its tortures seem
. . . valid . . . Reflections in a Golden Eye is the Southern
school at its most Gothic, but also at its best. It is as
though William Faulkner saw to the bottom of matters
which merely excite him, shed his stylistic faults, and
wrote it all out with Tolstoyan lucidity."

—Time

"ONE OF THE MOST COMPELLING,
MOST UNCANNY STORIES
EVER WRITTEN IN AMERICA."

—Louis Untermeyer

CARSON McCULLERS'
REFLECTIONS
IN A
GOLDEN EYE

With an Introduction
by TENNESSEE WILLIAMS

BANTAM BOOKS
NEW YORK · TORONTO · LONDON · SYDNEY · AUCKLAND

This edition contains the complete text
of the original hardcover edition.
NOT ONE WORD HAS BEEN OMITTED.

REFLECTIONS IN A GOLDEN EYE

A Bantam Book / published by arrangement
with Houghton Mifflin Company

PUBLISHING HISTORY

Houghton Mifflin edition published February 1941
Bantam editon / September 1950
Bantam reissue / November 1994

ISBN 0-553-56968-6

Published simultaneously in the United States and Canada

Bantam Books are published by Bantam Books, a division of Bantam
Doubleday Dell Publishing Group, Inc. Its trademark, consisting of
the words "Bantam Books" and the portrayal of a rooster, is Registered
in U.S. Patent and Trademark Office and in other countries. Marca
Registrada. Bantam Books, 1540 Broadway, New York, New York
10036.

PRINTED IN THE UNITED STATES OF AMERICA

RAD   0 9 8 7 6 5 4 3 2

Introduction

by Tennessee Williams

This book, *Reflections in a Golden Eye*, is a second novel, and although its appreciation has steadily risen during the years since its first appearance, it was then regarded as somewhat disappointing in the way that second novels usually are. When the book preceding a second novel has been very highly acclaimed, as was *The Heart Is a Lonely Hunter*, there is an inclination on the part of critics to retrench their favor, so nearly automatic and invariable a tendency that it can almost be set down as a physical law. But the reasons for failure to justly evaluate this second novel go beyond the common, temporal disadvantage that all second novels must suffer, and I feel that an examination of these reasons may be of considerably greater pertinence to our aim of suggesting a fresh evaluation.

To quote directly from book-notices is virtually impossible, here in Rome where I am writing these comments, but I believe that I am safe in assuming that it was their identification of the author with a certain school of American writers, mostly of Southern origin, that made her subject to a particular and powerful line of attack.

Even in the preceding book some readers must undoubtedly have detected a warning predisposition toward certain elements which are popularly known as 'morbid.' Doubtless there were some critics, as well as readers, who did not understand why Carson McCullers had elected to deal with a matter so unwholesome as the spiritual but passionate attachment that existed between a deaf-mute and a half-wit. But the tenderness of the book disarmed them. The depth and nobility of its compassion were so palpable that at least for the time being the charge of decadence had to be held in check. This forbearance was of short duration. In her second novel the veil of a subjective tenderness, which is the one quality of her talent which she has occasionally used to some excess, was drawn away. And the young writer suddenly flashed in their faces the cabalistic emblems of fellowship with a certain company of writers that the righteous 'Humanists' in the world of letters regarded as most abhorrent and most necessary to expose and attack.

Not being a follower of literary journals, I am not at all sure what title has been conferred upon this group of writers by their disparaging critics, but for my own convenience I will refer to them as the Gothic School. It has a very ancient lineage, this school, but our local inheritance of its tradition was first brought into prominence by the early novels of William Faulkner, who still remains a most notorious and unregenerate member. There is something in the region, something in the blood and culture, of the Southern state that has somehow made them the center of this Gothic school of writers. Certainly something more important than the influence of a single artist, Faulkner, is to be credited with its development, just as in France the Existentialist movement is surely attributable to forces more significant than the personal influence of Jean-Paul Sartre. There is actually a common link between the two schools, French and American, but characteristically the motor impulse of the French school is intellectual and philosophic while that of the American is more of an emotional and romantic nature. What is this common link? In my opinion it is most simply definable as a sense, an intuition, of an underlying dreadfulness in modern experience.

The question one hears most frequently about writers of the Gothic school is this little classic:

"Why do they write about such *dreadful* things?"

This is a question that escapes not only from the astonished lips of summer matrons who have stumbled into the odd world of William Faulkner, through some inadvertence or mischief at the lending-library, but almost as frequently and certainly more importantly, from the pens of some of the most eminent book-critics. If it were a solely and typically philistine manifestation, there would be no sense or hope in trying to answer it, but the fact that it is used as a major line of attack by elements that the artist has to deal with, critics, publishers, distributors, not to mention the reading public, makes it a question that we should try seriously to answer or at least understand.

The great difficulty of understanding, and communication, lies in the fact that we who are asked this question and those who ask it do not really inhabit the same universe.

You do not need to tell me that this remark smacks of artistic snobbism which is about as unattractive as any other form that snobbism can take. (If artists are snobs, it is much in the same humble way that lunatics are: not because they wish to be different, and hope and believe that they are, but because they are forever painfully struck in the face with the inescapable fact of their difference which makes them hurt and lonely enough to want to undertake the vocation of artists.)

It appears to me, sometimes, that there are only two kinds of people who live outside what E. E. Cummings has defined as "this socalled world of ours"—the artists and the insane. Of course there are those who are not practising artists and those who have not been committed to asylums, but who have enough of one or both magical elements, lunacy and vision, to permit them also to slip sufficiently apart from "this socalled world of ours" to undertake or accept an exterior view of it. But I feel that Mr. Cummings established a highly defensible point when he stated, at least by implication, that "the everyday humdrum world, which includes me and you and millions upon millions of men and women" is pretty largely something done with mirrors, and the mirrors are the millions of eyes that look at each other and things no more penetratingly than the physical senses allow. If they are conscious of there being anything to explore beyond this *soi-disant* universe, they comfortably suppose it to be represented by the mellow tones of the pipe-organ on Sundays.

In expositions of this sort it is sometimes very convenient to invent an opposite party to an argument, as Mr. Cummings did in making the remarks I have quoted. Such an invented adversary might say to me at this point:

"I have read some of these books, like this one here, and I think they're sickening and crazy. I don't know why anybody should want to write about such diseased and perverted and fantastic creatures and try to pass them off as representative members of the human race! That's how I feel about it. But I do have this sense you talk about, as much as you do or anybody else, this sense of fearfulness or dreadfulness or whatever you want to call it. I read the newspapers and I think it's all pretty awful. I think the atom bomb is awful and I think that the confusion of the world is awful. I think that cancer is fearful, and I certainly don't look forward to the idea of dying, which I think is dreadful. I could go on forever, or at least indefinitely, giving you a list of things that I think are dreadful. And isn't that having what you call the Sense of Dreadfulness or something?"

My hesitant answer would be—"Yes, and no. Mostly no."

And then I would explain a little further, with my usual awkwardness at exposition:

"All of these things that you list as dreadful are parts of the visible, sensible phenomena of every man's experience or knowledge, but the true sense of dread is not a reaction to anything sensible or visible or even, strictly, materially, *knowable*. But rather it's a kind of spiritual intuition of something almost too incredible and shocking to talk about, which underlies the whole so-called thing. It is the incommunicable something that we shall have to call *mystery* which is so inspiring of dread among these modern artists that we have been talking about. . . ."

Then I pause, looking into the eyes of my interlocutor which I hope are beginning to betray some desire to believe me, and I say to him, "Am I making any better sense?"

"Maybe. But I can see it's an effort!"

"My friend, you have me where the hair is short."

"But you know, you still haven't explained why these writers have to write about crazy people doing terrible things!"

"You mean the externals they use?"

" 'Externals?' "

"You are objecting to their choice of symbols."

"Symbols, are they?"

"Of course. Art is made out of symbols the way your body is made out of vital tissue."

"Then why have they got to use—?"

"Symbols of the grotesque and the violent? Because a book is short and a man's life is long."

"That I don't understand."

"Think it over."

"You mean it's got to be more concentrated?"

"Exactly. The awfulness has to be compressed."

"But can't a writer ever get the same effect without using such God damn awful subjects?"

"I believe one writer did. The greatest of modern times, James Joyce. He managed to get the whole sense of awfulness without resorting to externals that departed on the surface from the ordinary and the familiar. But he wrote very long books, when he accomplished this incredibly difficult thing, and also he used a device that is known as the interior monologue which only he and one other great modern writer could employ without being excessively tiresome."

"What other?"

"Marcel Proust. But Proust did not ever quite dare to deliver the message of Absolute Dread. He was too much of a physical coward. The atmosphere of his work is rather womb-like. The flight into protection is very apparent."

"I guess we've talked long enough. Don't you have to get back to your subject now?"

"I have just about finished with my subject, thanks to you."

"Aren't you going to make a sort of statement that adds it up?"

"Neatly? Yes. Maybe I'd better try: here it is: *Reflections in a Golden Eye* is one of the purest and most powerful of those works which are conceived in that Sense of The Awful which is the desperate black root of nearly all significant modern art, from the *Guernica* of Picasso to the cartoons of Charles Addams. Is that all right?"

"I have quit arguing with you. So long."

It is true that this book lacks somewhat the thematic magnitude of the *Chasseur Solitaire,* but there is an equally important respect in which it is superior.

The first novel had a tendency to overflow in places as if the virtuosity of the young writer had not yet fallen under her entire control. But in the second there is an absolute mastery of design. There is a lapidary precision about the structure of this second book. Furthermore I think it succeeds more perfectly in establishing its own reality, in creating a world of its own, and this is something that primarily distinguishes the work of a great artist from that of a professional writer. In this book there is perhaps no single passage that assaults the heart so mercilessly as that scene in the earlier novel where the deaf-mute Singer stands at night outside the squalid flat that he had formerly occupied with the crazed and now dying Antonapoulos. The acute tragic sensibility of scenes like that occurred more frequently in *The Heart Is a Lonely Hunter.* Here the artistic climate is more austere. The tragedy is more distilled: a Grecian purity cools it, the eventually overwhelming impact is of a more reflective order. The key to this deliberate difference is implicit in the very title of the book. Discerning critics should have found it the opposite of a disappointment since it exhibited the one attribute which had yet to be shown in Carson

McCullers' stunning array of gifts: the gift of mastery over a youthful lyricism.

I will add, however, that this second novel is still not her greatest; it is surpassed by *The Member of the Wedding*, her third novel, which combined the heart-breaking tenderness of the first with the sculptural quality of the second. But this book is in turn surpassed by a somewhat shorter work. I am speaking of *The Ballad of the Sad Cafe*, which is assuredly among the masterpieces of our language in the form of the novella.

During the two years that I have spent mostly abroad I have been impressed by the disparity that exists between Carson McCullers' reputation at home and in Europe. Translation serves as a winnowing process. The lesser and more derivative talents that have boisterously flooded our literary scene, with reputations inflated by professional politics and by shrewd commercial promotion, have somewhat obscured at home the position of more authentic talents. But in Europe the name of Carson McCullers is where it belongs, among the four or five preeminent figures in contemporary American writing.

Carson McCullers does not work rapidly. She is not coerced by the ridiculous popular idea that a good novelist turns out a book once a year. As long as five years elapsed between her second full-length novel and her third. I understand now that she has begun to work upon another. There could be no better literary news for any of us who have found, as I have found in her work, such intensity and nobility of spirit as we have not had in our prose-writing since Herman Melville. In the meantime she should be reassured by the constantly more abundant evidence that the work she has already accomplished, such as this work, is not eclipsed by time but further illumined.

Tennessee Williams

i

An army post in peacetime is a dull place. Things happen, but then they happen over and over again. The general plan of a fort in itself adds to the monotony—the huge concrete barracks, the neat rows of officers' homes built one precisely like the other, the gym, the chapel, the golf course and the swimming pools—all is designed according to a certain rigid pattern. But perhaps the dullness of a post is caused most of all by insularity and by a surfeit of leisure and safety, for once a man enters

the army he is expected only to follow the heels
ahead of him. At the same time things do occasionally happen on an army post that are not likely to
re-occur. There is a fort in the South where a few
years ago a murder was committed. The partici-
pants of this tragedy were: two officers, a soldier,
two women, a Filipino, and a horse.

The soldier in this affair was Private Ellgee Williams. Often in the late afternoon he could be seen
sitting alone on one of the benches that lined the
sidewalk before the barracks. This was a pleasant
place, as here there was a long double row of
young maple trees that patterned the lawn and the
walk with cool, delicate, windblown shadows. In
the spring the leaves of the trees were a lucent
green that as the hot months came took on a
darker, restful hue. In late autumn they were
flaming gold. Here Private Williams would sit and
wait for the call to evening mess. He was a silent
young soldier and in the barracks he had neither
an enemy nor a friend. His round sunburned face
was marked by a certain watchful innocence. His
full lips were red and the bangs of his hair lay
brown and matted on his forehead. In his eyes,
which were of a curious blend of amber and
brown, there was a mute expression that is found
usually in the eyes of animals. At first glance Private Williams seemed a bit heavy and awkward in
his bearing. But this was a deceptive impression;
he moved with the silence and agility of a wild

creature or a thief. Often soldiers who had thought themselves alone were startled to see him appear as from nowhere by their sides. His hands were small, delicately boned, and very strong.

Private Williams did not smoke, drink, fornicate, or gamble. In the barracks he kept to himself and was something of a mystery to the other men. Most of his leisure time Private Williams spent out in the woods surrounding the post. The reservation, fifteen miles square, was wild unspoiled country. Here were to be found giant virgin pines, many varieties of flowers, and even such shy animals as deer, wild pig, and foxes. Except for riding, Private Williams cared for none of the sports available to enlisted men. No one had ever seen him in the gym or at the swimming pool. Nor had he ever been known to laugh, to become angry, or to suffer in any way. He ate three wholesome, bounteous meals a day and never grumbled about the food as did the other soldiers. He slept in a room accommodating a long double row of about three dozen cots. This was not a peaceful room. At night when the lights were out there was often the sound of snores, of curses, and of strangled nightmare groans. But Private Williams rested tranquilly. Only sometimes from his cot there would be a stealthy rustle from the wrapper of a candy bar.

When Private Williams had been in the army for two years he was sent one day to the quarters of a certain Captain Penderton. This came about in the following manner. For the past six months Private Williams had been detailed to permanent stable fatigue, as he was quite a hand with horses. Captain Penderton had telephoned the post Sergeant Major and by chance, as many of the horses were out on maneuvers and work around the stables was slack, Private Williams was chosen for this particular duty. The nature of the assignment was simple. Captain Penderton wished a small part of the woods behind his quarters cleared so that later when a steak grill was put up he could give alfresco parties. This job would require about one full day's work.

Private Williams set out for this assignment at about seven-thirty in the morning. It was a mild and sunny day in October. He knew already where the Captain lived, as he had passed his house often when starting out for his walks in the woods. Also, he knew the Captain well by sight. In fact he had once done the Captain an accidental injury. A year and a half ago Private Williams had for a few weeks served as striker to the Lieutenant in command of the company to which he was then attached. One afternoon the Lieutenant received a visit from Captain Penderton and while serving them refreshments Private Williams had spilled a cup of coffee on the Captain's trousers. In addition to this he now saw the Captain frequently at the stables and he had in his charge the horse of the

Captain's wife—a chestnut stallion which was easily the handsomest mount on the post.

The Captain lived on the outskirts of the fort. His house, an eight-room two-story building of stucco, was identical with all the other houses on the street except for the distinction of being an end house. On two sides the lawn adjoined the forest of the reservation. On the right the Captain had as his only near neighbor Major Morris Langdon. The houses on this street faced a large, flat expanse of brown sward which had until recently served as the polo field.

When Private Williams arrived, the Captain came out to explain in detail what he wanted done. The scrub oaks, the low briary bushes were to be cleared, the limbs of the large trees growing at a level less than six feet would be cut away. The Captain pointed out a large old oak about twenty yards from the lawn as the boundary for the space to be worked on. The Captain wore a gold ring on one of his white, fattish hands. He was dressed this morning in knee-length khaki shorts, high wool socks, and a suede jacket. His face was sharp and strained. He had black hair and eyes of a glassy blue. The Captain did not seem to recognize Private Williams and he gave his directions in a nervous, finicky manner. He told Private Williams he wanted the work completed that day and said he would be back sometime in the late afternoon.

The soldier worked steadily all morning. At noon

he went to the mess hall for his lunch. By four o'clock the job was finished. He had done even more than the Captain specifically requested. The large oak marking the boundary had an unusual shape—the branches on the side toward the lawn were high enough to walk beneath, but the branches on the opposite side swept down gracefully to the ground. The soldier had with a great deal of trouble cut off these down-sweeping limbs. Then, when all was done, he leaned against the trunk of a pine tree to wait. He seemed at peace with himself and quite content to stand there waiting forever.

'Why, what are *you* doing here?' a voice asked him suddenly.

The soldier had seen the Captain's wife come out of the rear entrance of the house next door and walk toward him across the lawn. He saw her, but she did not enter the dark sphere of his consciousness until she spoke to him.

'I was just down at the stables,' Mrs. Penderton said. 'My Firebird has been kicked.'

'Yes, ma'am,' the soldier answered vaguely. He waited for a moment to digest the meaning of her words. 'How?'

'That I don't know. Maybe some damn mule or maybe they let him in with the mares. I was mad about it and I asked for you.'

The Captain's wife lay down in a hammock that was slung between two trees on the edge of the lawn. Even in the clothes she was now wearing—boots, soiled whipcord breeches very worn at the knees, and a gray jersey—she was a handsome woman. Her face had the bemused placidity of a Madonna's and she wore her straight bronze hair brought back in a knot at the nape of her neck. As she was resting there the servant, a young Negress, came out with a tray holding a pint bottle of rye, a whiskey jigger, and some water. Mrs. Penderton was not pernickety about her liquor. She drank down two jiggers straight and chased them with a swallow of cold water. She did not speak to the soldier again and he did not question her further about the horse. Neither seemed aware of the presence of the other in any way. The soldier leaned back against his pine tree and stared unblinking into space.

The late autumn sun laid a radiant haze over the new sodded winter grass of the lawn, and even in the woods the sun shone through in places where the leaves were not so dense, to make fiery golden patterns on the ground. Then suddenly the sun was gone. There was a chill in the air and a light, pure wind. It was time for retreat. From far away came the sound of the bugle, clarified by distance and echoing in the woods with a lost hollow tone. The night was near at hand.

At this point Captain Penderton returned. He parked his car before the house and crossed the yard immediately to see how the work had been

done. He greeted his wife and curtly saluted the
soldier who now stood at rather lax attention before him. The Captain glanced over the cleared
space. All at once he snapped his fingers and his
lips sharpened with a thin, stiff sneer. He turned
his light blue eyes to the soldier. Then he said very
quietly: 'Private, the whole idea was in the big oak
tree.'

The soldier received his comment in silence. His
round serious face did not change.

'The instructions were for the ground to be
cleared only so far as the oak tree,' the officer continued in a higher voice. Stiffly he walked back to
the tree in question and pointed to the cut stark
limbs. 'The way the boughs swept down and made
a background shutting off the rest of the woods
was the whole point. Now it is all ruined.' The
Captain's agitation seemed more than such a mishap warranted. Standing alone in the woods he
was a small man.

'What does the Captain want me to do?' Private
Williams asked after a long pause.

Mrs. Penderton laughed suddenly and put down
one booted foot to rock the hammock. 'The Captain wants you to pick up the branches and sew
them back on again.'

Her husband was not amused. 'Here!' he said to
the soldier. 'Bring some leaves and spread them on
the ground to cover the bare spaces where the

bushes have been cleared. Then you may go.' He tipped the soldier and went into the house.

Private Williams walked slowly back into the darkened woods to gather fallen leaves. The Captain's wife rocked herself and seemed about to go to sleep. The sky filled with a pale, cold yellow light and all was still.

Captain Penderton was in no comfortable state of mind this evening. On coming into the house he went straight to his study. This was a small room planned originally as a sun porch and leading from the dining-room. The Captain settled himself at his desk and opened a thick notebook. He spread out a map before him and took his slide rule from a drawer. In spite of these preparations he was unable to put his mind to his work. He leaned over the desk with his head in his hands and his eyes closed.

In part his restlessness was caused by his annoyance with Private Williams. He had been irritated when he saw that it was this particular soldier who had been sent him. There were perhaps only half a dozen enlisted men on all the post whose faces were familiar to the Captain. He looked on all soldiers with bored contempt. To him officers and men might belong to the same biological genus, but they were of an altogether different species. The Captain well remembered the accident of the spilled coffee, as it had ruined for him a brand-new

and costly outfit. The suit was of heavy Chinese silk
and the stain had never been entirely removed.
(The Captain always wore uniform when away
from the post, but on all social occasions among
other officers he affected mufti and was a great
swell.) Aside from this grievance Private Williams
was associated in the Captain's mind with the stables and his wife's horse, Firebird—an unpleasant
association. And now the blunder about the oak
tree was the last straw. Sitting at his desk the Captain indulged in a brief, peevish daydream—he imagined a fantastic situation in which he caught the
soldier transgressing in some way and was instru-
mental in having him court-martialed. This con-
soled him a little. He poured himself a cup of tea
from the thermos bottle on his desk and became
absorbed in other and more pertinent worries.

The Captain's restlessness this evening had many
causes. His personality differed in some respects
from the ordinary. He stood in a somewhat curious
relation to the three fundaments of existence—life
itself, sex, and death. Sexually the Captain obtained within himself a delicate balance between
the male and female elements, with the susceptibil-
ities of both the sexes and the active powers of neither. For a person content to withdraw a bit from
life, and able to collect his scattered passions and
throw himself wholeheartedly into some impersonal work, some art or even some crack-brained
fixed idea such as an attempt to square the

circle—for such a person this state of being is
bearable enough. The Captain had his work and
he did not spare himself; it was said that he had a
brilliant career ahead of him. Perhaps he would
not have felt this basic lack, or superfluity, if it had
not been for his wife. But with her he suffered. He
had a sad penchant for becoming enamoured of his
wife's lovers.

As to his relations with the other two fundaments, his position was simple enough. In his balance between the two great instincts, toward life
and toward death, the scale was heavily weighted
to one side—to death. Because of this the Captain
was a coward.

Captain Penderton was also something of a sa-
vant. During the years when he was a young Lieutenant and a bachelor he had had much opportunity to read, as his fellow officers tended to avoid his
room in the bachelors' quarters or else to visit him
in pairs or groups. His head was filled with statis-
tics and information of scholarly exactitude. For instance, he could describe in detail the curious
digestive apparatus of a lobster or the life history
of a Trilobite. He spoke and wrote three languages
gracefully. He knew something of astronomy and
had read much poetry. But in spite of his knowledge of many separate facts, the Captain never in
his life had had an idea in his head. For the forma-
tion of an idea involves the fusion of two or more

known facts. And this the Captain had not the courage to do.

As he sat alone at his desk this evening, unable to work, he did not question himself as to his feelings. He thought again of the face of Private Williams. Then he recollected that the Langdons next door were dining with them that evening. Major Morris Langdon was his wife's lover, but the Captain did not dwell on this. Instead he suddenly remembered an evening long ago, soon after he had married. On that evening he had felt this same unhappy restlessness and had seen fit to relieve himself in a curious manner. He had driven into a town near the post where he was then stationed, had parked his car, and had walked for a long time in the streets. It was a late winter night. In the course of this walk the Captain came upon a tiny kitten hovered in a doorway. The kitten had found shelter and made itself warm; when the Captain leaned down he found that it was purring. He picked up the kitten and felt it vibrate in his palm. For a long time he looked into the soft, gentle little face and stroked the warm fur. The kitten was at the age when it was first able to open wide its clear green eyes. At last the Captain had taken the kitten with him down the street. On the corner there was a mailbox and after one quick glance around him he had opened the freezing letter slot and squeezed the kitten inside. Then he had continued on his way.

The Captain heard the back door slam and he left his desk. In the kitchen his wife sat on a table while Susie, the colored servant, pulled off her boots. Mrs. Penderton was not a pure-bred Southerner. She had been born and brought up in the army, and her father, who a year before his retirement had reached the rank of Brigadier General, was originally from the West coast. Her mother, however, had been a South Carolinian. And in her ways the Captain's wife was Southern enough. Their gas stove was not crusted with generations of dirt as her grandmother's had been, but then it was by no means clean. Mrs. Penderton also held to many other old Southern notions, such as the belief that pastry or bread is not fit to eat unless it is rolled on a marble-topped table. For this reason they had once, when the Captain was detailed to Schofield Barracks, hauled the table on which she was now sitting all the way to Hawaii and back. If the Captain's wife chanced to find a black, crooked hair in her food, she wiped it calmly on her napkin and went right on with the enjoyment of her dinner without the bat of an eye.

'Susie,' said Mrs. Penderton, 'do people have gizzards like chickens do?'

The Captain stood in the doorway and was noticed neither by his wife nor his servant. When she had been relieved of her boots, Mrs. Penderton moved about the kitchen bare-footed. She took a ham from the oven and sprinkled the top with brown sugar and bread crumbs. She poured herself another drink, only half a jigger this time, and in a sudden excess of vigor she performed a little shag dance. The Captain was intensely irritated with his wife, and she knew it.

'For God's sake, Leonora, go up and put on some shoes.'

For an answer Mrs. Penderton hummed a queer little tune to herself and went past the Captain and into the living-room.

Her husband followed close behind her. 'You look like a slattern going around the house like this.'

A fire was laid in the grate and Mrs. Penderton bent down to light it. Her smooth sweet face was very rosy and there were little glistening sweat beads on her upper lip.

'The Langdons are coming any minute now and you will sit down to dinner like this, I suppose?'

'Sure,' she said. 'And why not, you old prissy?'

The Captain said in a cold, taut voice: 'You disgust me.'

Mrs. Penderton's answer was a sudden laugh, a laugh both soft and savage, as though she had received some long expected piece of scandalous news or had thought of some sly joke. She pulled off her jersey, crushed it into a ball, and threw it into the corner of the room. Then deliberately she unbuttoned her breeches and stepped out of them. In a moment she was standing naked by the

hearth. Before the bright gold and orange light of
the fire her body was magnificent. The shoulders
were straight so that the collar bone made a sharp
pure line. Between her round breasts there were
delicate blue veins. In a few years her body would
be fullblown like a rose with loosened petals, but
now the soft roundness was controlled and disci-
plined by sport. Although she stood quite still and
placid, there was about her body a subtle quality
of vibration, as though on touching her flesh one
would feel the slow live coursing of the bright
blood beneath. While the Captain looked at her
with the stunned indignation of a man who has
suffered a slap in the face, she walked serenely to
the vestibule on her way to the stairs. The front
door was open and from the dark night outside a
breeze blew in and lifted a loose strand of her
bronze hair.

She was halfway up the steps before the Captain
recovered from his shock. Then he ran trembling
after her. 'I will kill you!' he said in a strangled
voice. 'I will do it! I will do it!' He crouched with
his hand to the banister and one foot on the second
step of the stairway as though ready to spring up
after her.

She turned slowly and looked down at him with
unconcern for a moment before she spoke. 'Son,
have you ever been collared and dragged out in
the street and thrashed by a naked woman?'

The Captain stood as she had left him. Then he

put his head down on his outstretched arm and rested his weight against the banister. From his throat came a rasping sound like a sob, but there were no tears on his face. After a time he stood up and wiped his neck with his handkerchief. Only then did he notice that the front door was open, the house brightly lighted, and all the shades raised. He felt himself sicken strangely. Anyone might have passed along the dark street before the house. He thought of the soldier whom he had left a short while ago on the edge of the woods. Even he might have seen what had occurred. The Captain looked all about him with frightened eyes. Then he went into his study where he kept a decanter of old, strong brandy.

Leonora Penderton feared neither man, beast, nor the devil; God she had never known. At the very mention of the Lord's name she thought only of her old father who had sometimes read the Bible on a Sunday afternoon. Of that book she remembered two things clearly: one, that Jesus had been crucified at a place called Cavalry Hill—the other, that once He had ridden somewhere on a jackass, and what sort of person would want to ride a jackass?

Within five minutes Leonora Penderton had forgotten the scene with her husband. She ran the water for her bath and laid out her clothes for the evening. Leonora Penderton was the subject of much lively gossip among the ladies of the post.

According to them her past and present affairs were a rich medley of amorous exploits. But most of what these ladies told was hearsay and conjecture—for Leonora Penderton was a person who liked to settle herself and was adverse to complications. When she married the Captain she had been a virgin. Four nights after her wedding she was still a virgin, and on the fifth night her status was changed only enough to leave her somewhat puzzled. As for the rest it would be hard to say. She herself would probably have reckoned her affairs according to a system of her own—giving the old Colonel at Leavenworth only half a count and the young Lieutenant in Hawaii several units in her calculations. But now for the past two years there had been only Major Morris Langdon and no one else. With him she was content.

On the post Leonora Penderton enjoyed a reputation as a good hostess, an excellent sportswoman, and even as a great lady. However, there was something about her that puzzled her friends and acquaintances. They sensed an element in her personality that they could not quite put their fingers on. The truth of the matter was that she was a little feebleminded.

This sad fact did not reveal itself at parties, or in the stables, or at her dinner table. There were only three persons who understood this: her old father, the General, who had worried no little about it until she was safely married; her husband, who

looked on it as a condition natural to all women
under forty; and Major Morris Langdon, who
loved her for it all the more. She could not have
multiplied twelve by thirteen under threat of the
rack. If ever it was strictly necessary that she write
a letter, such as a note to thank her uncle for a
birthday check or a letter ordering a new bridle, it
was a weighty enterprise for her. She and Susie
shut themselves in the kitchen with scholarly seclu-
sion. They sat down to a table furnished with an
abundance of paper and several nicely sharpened
pencils. Then, when the final draft was finished
and copied, they were both exhausted and in great
need of a quiet, restoring drink.

Leonora Penderton enjoyed her warm bath that
evening. She dressed herself slowly in the clothes
she had already laid out on the bed. She wore a
simple gray skirt, a blue Angora sweater, and pearl
earrings. She was downstairs again at seven o'clock
and their guests were waiting.

She and the Major found the dinner first-rate. To
begin with there was a clear soup. Then with the
ham they had rich oily turnip greens, and candied
sweet potatoes that were a transparent amber, beneath the light and richly glazed with sweet sauce.
There were rolls and hot spoon-bread. Susie passed
the vegetables only once and left the serving dishes
on the table between the Major and Leonora, for
those two were great eaters. The Major sat with
one elbow on the table and was altogether very

much at home. His red-brown face had a blunt,
jovial, and friendly expression; among both officers
and men he was very popular. Except for the mention of Firebird's accident there was almost no ta-
ble-talk. Mrs. Langdon hardly touched her dinner.
She was a small, dark, fragile woman with a large
nose and a sensitive mouth. She was very ill and
she looked it. Not only was this illness physical,
but she had been tortured to the bone by grief and
anxiety so that now she was on the verge of actual
lunacy. Captain Penderton sat very straight with
his elbows held close to his sides. Once he cor-
dially congratulated the Major on a medal he had
received. Several times during the course of the
meal he flicked the rim of his water goblet and listened to the clear, resonant ring. The dinner ended
with a dessert of hot mince pie. Then the four of
them went into the sitting-room to finish out the
evening with cards and conversation.

'My dear, you are a damn fine cook,' the Major
said comfortably.

The four people at the table had not been alone.
In the autumn darkness outside the window there
stood a man who watched them in silence. The
night was cold and the clean scent of pine trees
sharpened the air. A wind sang in the forest
near-by. The sky glittered with icy stars. The man
who watched them stood so close to the window
that his breath showed on the cold glass pane.

Private Williams had indeed seen Mrs. Penderton as she left the hearth and walked upstairs to her bath. And never before in his life had this young soldier seen a naked woman. He had been brought up in a household exclusively male. From his father, who ran a one-mule farm and preached on Sunday at a Holiness church, he had learned that women carried in them a deadly and catching disease which made men blind, crippled, and doomed to hell. In the army he also heard much talk of this bad sickness and was even himself examined once a month by the doctor to see if he had touched a woman. Private Williams had never willingly touched, or looked at, or spoken to a female since he was eight years old.

He had been late in gathering the armfuls of damp, rank autumn leaves back in the woods. When at last his duty was done, he had crossed the Captain's lawn on his way to evening mess. By chance he glanced into the sharply lighted vestibule. And since then he had not found it in him to go away. He stood motionless in the silent night with his arms hanging loose at his sides. When at dinner the ham was carved, he had swallowed painfully. But he kept his grave, deep gaze on the Captain's wife. The expression of his mute face had not been changed by his experience, but now and then he narrowed his gold-brown eyes as though he were forming within himself some subtle scheme. When the Captain's wife had left the dining-room, he still stood there for a time. Then very slowly he turned away. The light behind him laid a great dim shadow of himself on the smooth grass of the lawn. The soldier walked like a man weighted by a dark dream and his footsteps were soundless.

ii

Very early the next morning Private Williams went to the stables. The sun had not yet risen and the air was colorless and cold. Milky ribbons of mist clung to the damp earth and the sky was silver-gray. The path leading to the stables passed a bluff which commanded a sweeping view of the reservation. The woods were in full autumn color, and scattered among the blackish green of the pine trees there were blunt splashes of crimson and yellow. Private Williams walked slowly along the leafy path. Now and then he stopped altogether and stood perfectly still, in the attitude of one who listens to a call from a long distance. His sun-browned skin was flushed in the morning air and on his lips there were still the white traces of the milk he had drunk for breakfast. Loitering and stopping in this way he reached the stables just as the sun came up in the sky.

Inside the stable it was still almost dark and no one was about. The air was close, warm, and sour-sweet. As the soldier passed between the stalls he heard the placid breath of the horses, a sleepy snuffle and a whinny. Dumb, luminous eyes turned toward him. The young soldier took from his pocket an envelope of sugar and soon his hands were warm and sticky with slaver. He went into the stall of a little mare who was almost ready to drop her foal. He stroked her swollen belly and stood for a time with his arms around her neck. Then he let the mules out into their pen. The soldier was not alone with the beasts—soon the other men reported for their duty. It was Saturday, a busy day at the stables, as in the morning there were riding classes for the children and women of the post. The stable was soon noisy with talk and heavy footsteps; the horses grew restive in their stalls.

Mrs. Penderton was one of the first riders to come this morning. With her, as often, was Major Langdon. Captain Penderton accompanied them

today, which was unusual, as he customarily took
his ride alone and in the late afternoon. The three
of them sat on the paddock fence while their
mounts were being saddled. Private Williams led
out Firebird first. The injury of which the Captain's wife complained the day before had been
greatly exaggerated. On the horse's left foreleg
there was a slight abrasion that had been painted
with iodine. On being led out into the bright sunlight, the horse rounded his nostrils nervously and
turned his long neck to look about him. His coat
was curried smooth as satin and his mane was
thick and glossy in the sun.

At first glance the horse seemed overgrown and
too heavy-set for a thoroughbred. His great
haunches were broad and fleshy, and his legs were
somewhat thick. But he moved with marvelous,
fiery grace, and once at Camden he had outraced
his own great sire who was a champion. When
Mrs. Penderton was mounted, he reared up twice
and tried to break away toward the bridle path.
Then, straining against the bit, with arched neck
and tail raised high, he side-stepped furiously and
a light froth of foam showed on his muzzle. During
this struggle between horse and rider, Mrs. Penderton laughed aloud and spoke to Firebird in a voice
that was vibrant with passion and excitement: 'You
sweet old bastard, you!' The struggle ended as
abruptly as it had begun. Indeed, as this volatile
fracas took place every morning, it could hardly be

called a real struggle any longer. When the horse, as an ill-trained two-year-old, had first come to the stables, it had been earnest enough. Twice Mrs. Penderton was badly thrown, and once when she returned from her ride the soldiers saw that she had bitten her lower lip quite through so that there was blood on her sweater and shirt.

But now this brief daily struggle had a theatrical, affected air—it was a jocular pantomime performed for their own amusement and for the benefit of spectators. Even when the froth showed on his mouth, the horse moved with a certain fractious grace as though aware of being watched. And after it was over he stood quite still and sighed once, in much the same manner as a young husband would sigh laughingly and shrug his shoulders when giving in to the will of a beloved and termagant wife. Except for these mock rebellions the horse was now perfectly trained.

To all the regular riders the soldiers at the stables had given nicknames that they used when speaking among themselves. Major Langdon was called The Buffalo. This was because when in the saddle he slumped his great heavy shoulders and lowered his head. The Major was a fine horseman and, when a young Lieutenant, he had made a rare name for himself on the polo field. On the other hand, Captain Penderton was no rider at all, although he himself was not aware of this. He sat rigid as a ramrod in the exact position taught by the riding master. Perhaps he would not have ridden at all if he could have seen himself from the rear. His buttocks spread and jounced flabbily in the saddle. For this reason he was known to the soldiers as Captain Flap-Fanny. Mrs. Penderton was called simply The Lady, so great was the esteem in which she was held at the stables.

This morning the three riders started at a sedate walk, Mrs. Penderton leading. Private Williams stood watching them until they were out of sight. Soon he heard from the ring of the horses' hoofs on the hard path that they had broken into a canter. The sun was brighter now and the sky had darkened to a warm, brilliant blue. In the fresh air there was the odor of dung and burning leaves. The soldier stood so long that at last the Sergeant came up to him and roared good-naturedly: 'Hey, Unconscious, you mean to gawk there forever?' The sound of the horses' hoofs could be heard no longer. The young soldier pushed back his bangs from his forehead and slowly set about his work. He did not speak all day.

Then late in the evening Private Williams dressed in fresh clothes and went out to the woods. He walked along the edge of the reservation until he reached the stretch of woods he had cleared for Captain Penderton. The house was not brightly lighted as it had been before. Lights showed only in one room to the right upstairs, and in the small porch leading from the dining-room. When the soldier approached, he found the Captain in his study alone; the Captain's wife, then, was in the lighted room upstairs where the shades were drawn. The house, like all the houses on the block, was new, so that there had been no time for shrubs to grow in the yard. But the Captain had had twelve ligustrum trees transplanted and put in rows along the sides so that the place would not seem so raw and bare. Shielded by these thick-leaved evergreens, the soldier could not easily be seen from the street or the house next door. He stood so close to the Captain that if the window had been open he could have reached out and touched him with his hand.

Captain Penderton sat at his desk with his back turned to Private Williams. He was in a constant fidget as he studied. Besides the books and papers on his desk there was a purple glass decanter, a thermos bottle of tea, and a box of cigarettes. He drank hot tea and red wine. Every ten or fifteen minutes he put a new cigarette in his amber cigarette holder. He worked until two o'clock and the soldier watched him.

From this night there began a strange time. The soldier returned each evening, approaching by way of the forest, and looked at all that went on within the Captain's house. At the windows of the dining- and sitting-rooms there were lace curtains through which he could see, but not easily be seen himself. He stood to the side of the window, looking in obliquely, and the light did not fall on his face. Nothing of much consequence happened inside. Often they spent the evening away from home and did not return until after midnight. Once they entertained six guests at dinner. Most evenings, however, they spent with Major Langdon, who came either alone or with his wife. They would drink, play cards, and talk in the sitting-room. The soldier kept his eyes on the Captain's wife.

During this time a change was noticed in Private Williams. His new habit of suddenly stopping and looking for a long time into space was still with him. He would be cleaning out a stall or saddling a mule when all at once he seemed to withdraw into a trance. He would stand immovable and sometimes he did not even realize when his name was called. The Sergeant at the stables noticed this and was uneasy. He had occasionally seen this same queer habit in young soldiers who have grown homesick for the farm and womenfolk, and who plan to 'go over the hill.' But when the Sergeant questioned Private Williams, he answered that he was thinking about nothing at all.

The young soldier spoke the truth. Although his face wore an expression of still concentration, there were in his mind no plans or thoughts of which he was aware. In him was a deep reflection of the sight he had seen that night when passing before the Captain's lighted vestibule. But he did not think actively of The Lady or of anything else.

However, it was necessary for him to pause and wait in this trancelike attitude, for far down in his mind there had begun a dark, slow germination.

Four times in his twenty years of life the soldier had acted of his own accord and without the pressure of immediate circumstance. Each of these four actions had been preceded by these same odd trances. The first of these actions was the sudden, inexplicable purchase of a cow. By the time he was a boy of seventeen, he had accumulated a hundred dollars by plowing and picking cotton. With this money he had bought this cow, and he named her Ruby Jewel. There was no need on his father's one-mule farm for a cow. It was unlawful for them to sell the milk, for their makeshift stable would not pass government inspection, and the milk that she yielded was far more than their small household could use. On winter mornings the boy would get up before daylight and go out with a lantern to his cow's stall. He would press his forehead against her warm flank as he milked and talk to her in soft, urgent whispers. He put his cupped hands down into the pail of frothy milk and drank with lingering swallows.

The second of these actions was a sudden, violent declaration of his faith in the Lord. He always had sat quietly on one of the back benches of the church where his father preached on Sunday. But one night during a revival he suddenly leaped up onto the platform. He called to God with strange wild sounds and rolled in convulsions on the floor. Afterward he had been very languid for a week and he never again found the spirit in this way.

The third of these actions was a crime which he committed and successfully concealed. And the fourth was his enlistment in the army.

Each of these happenings had come about very suddenly and without any conscious planning on his part. Still in a curious way, he had prepared for them. For instance, just before the purchase of his cow he had stood gazing into space for a long while and then he cleaned out a lean-to by the barn that had been used for storing junk; when he brought home the cow there was a place ready for her. In the same manner he had got his small affairs in order before his enlistment. But he did not actually know that he was going to buy a cow until he counted out his money and put his hand on the halter. And it was only as he stepped over the threshold of the enlistment office that the vaporish impressions within him condensed to a thought, so that he realized he would be a soldier.

For almost two weeks Private Williams reconnoitered in this secret manner around the Captain's quarters. He learned the habits of the household. The servant was usually in bed at ten o'clock. When Mrs. Penderton spent the evening at home, she went upstairs at about eleven and the light in

her room was turned off. As a rule the Captain
worked from about ten-thirty until two o'clock.

Then on the twelfth night the soldier walked
through the woods even more slowly than usual.
From a far distance he saw that the house was
lighted. In the sky there was a white brilliant moon
and the night was cold and silvery. The soldier
could be plainly seen as he left the woods to cross
the lawn. In his right hand was a pocket-knife and
he had changed his clumsy boots for tennis shoes.
From the sitting-room there was the sound of
voices. The soldier went up to the window.

'Hit me, Morris,' said Leonora Penderton. 'Give
me a big number this time.'

Major Langdon and the Captain's wife were
playing a game of blackjack. The stakes were
worth while and their system of reckoning very
simple. If the Major won all the chips on the table,
he was to have Firebird for a week—if Leonora
won them, she would get a bottle of her favorite
rye. During the last hour the Major had raked in
most of the chips. The firelight reddened his handsome face and he was drumming a military tattoo
with the heel of his boot on the floor. His black
hair was turning white at the temples; already his
clipped mustache was a becoming gray. Tonight
he was in uniform. His heavy shoulders were
slouched and he seemed warmly contented except
when he glanced over at his wife—then his light
eyes were uneasy and beseeching. Across from him

Leonora had a studious, serious air, as she was trying to add fourteen and seven on her fingers underneath the table. At last she put the cards down.

'Am I busted?'

'No, my dear,' said the Major. 'Twenty-one exactly. Blackjack.'

Captain Penderton and Mrs. Langdon sat before the hearth. Neither of them was comfortable at all. They were both nervous this evening and had been talking with grim vivacity about gardening. There were good reasons for their nervousness. These days the Major was not altogether the same easy-go-lucky man he used to be. And even Leonora vaguely felt the general depression. For one reason, a strange and tragic thing had happened among these four people a few months ago. They had been sitting like this late one night when suddenly Mrs. Langdon, who had a high temperature, left the room and ran over to her own house. The Major did not follow her immediately, as he was comfortably stupefied with whiskey. Then later Anacleto, the Langdons' Filipino servant, rushed wailing into the room with such a wild-eyed face that they followed him without a word. They found Mrs. Langdon unconscious and she had cut off the tender nipples of her breasts with the garden shears.

'Does anybody want a drink?' the Captain asked.

They were all thirsty, and the Captain went back to the kitchen for another bottle of soda

water. His deep uneasiness of mind was caused by
the fact that he knew things could not go on much
longer as they were. And although the affair between his wife and Major Langdon had been a torment to him, he could not think of any likely
change without dread. Indeed his torment had
been a rather special one, as he was just as jealous
of his wife as he was of her lover. In the last year
he had come to feel an emotional regard for the
Major that was the nearest thing to love that he
had ever known. More than anything else he
longed to distinguish himself in the eyes of this
man. He carried his cuckoldry with a cynical good
grace that was respected on the post. Now as he
poured out the Major's drink his hand was shaking.

'You work too hard, Weldon,' Major Langdon
said. 'And let me tell you one thing—it's not worth
it. Your health comes first because where would
you be if you lost it? Leonora, do you want another
card?'

As Captain Penderton poured Mrs. Langdon's
drink, he avoided her eyes. He loathed her so
much that he could scarcely bear to look at her.
She sat very quiet and stiff before the fire and she
was knitting. Her face was deadly pale and her lips
were rather swollen and chapped. She had soft,
black eyes of feverish brilliance. She was twenty-
nine years old, two years younger than Leonora. It
was said that she once had had a beautiful voice,
but no one on this post had ever heard her sing. As

the Captain looked at her hands, he felt a quiver of nausea. Her hands were slender to the point of emaciation, with long fragile fingers and delicate branchings of greenish veins from the knuckles to the wrist. They were sickly pale against the crimson wool of the sweater she was knitting. Frequently, in many mean and subtle ways, the Captain tried to hurt this woman. He disliked her first of all because of her total indifference to himself. The Captain despised her also for the fact that she had done him a service—she knew, and kept secret, a matter which if gossiped about could cause him the most distressing embarrassment.

'Another sweater for your husband?'

'No,' she said quietly. 'I haven't decided just what I mean to do with this.'

Alison Langdon wanted terribly to cry. She had been thinking of her baby, Catherine, who had died three years before. She knew that she should go home and let her houseboy, Anacleto, help her get to bed. She was in pain and nervous. Even the fact that she did not know for whom she was knitting this sweater was a source of irritation to her. She had taken to knitting only when she had learned about her husband. At first she had done a number of sweaters for him. Then she had knitted a suit for Leonora. During the first months she could not quite believe that he could be so faithless to her. When at last she had scornfully given up her husband, she had turned desperately to

Leonora. There began one of those peculiar friend-
ships between the wife who has been betrayed and
the object of her husband's love. This morbid, emotional attachment, bastard of shock and jealousy,
she knew was unworthy of her. Of its own accord
it had soon ended. Now she felt the tears come to
her eyes and she drank a little whiskey to brace
herself, although liquor was forbidden her because
of her heart. She herself did not even like the taste
of it. She much preferred a tiny glass of some syr-
upy liqueur, or a little sherry, or even a cup of
coffee if it came to that. But now she drank the
whiskey because it was there, and the others were
drinking, and there was nothing else to do.

'Weldon!' called out the Major suddenly, 'your
wife is cheating! She peeked under the card to find
if she wanted it.'

'No, I didn't. You caught me before I had a
chance to see it. What have you got there?'

'I'm surprised at you, Morris,' said Captain Penderton. 'Don't you know you can never trust a
woman at cards?'

Mrs. Langdon watched this friendly badinage
with an on-the-defensive expression that is often
seen in the eyes of persons who have been ill for a
long time and dependent upon the thoughtfulness,
or negligence, of others. Since the night she had
rushed home and hurt herself, she had felt in her a
constant, nauseous shame. She was sure that everyone who looked at her must be thinking of what

she had done. But as a matter of fact the scandal
had been kept quite secret; besides those in the
room only the doctor and the nurse knew what had
happened—and the young Filipino servant who
had been with Mrs. Langdon since he was seventeen years old and who adored her. Now she
stopped knitting and put the tips of her fingers to
her cheekbones. She knew that she should get up
and leave the room, and break with her husband
altogether. But lately she had been overcome by a
terrible helplessness. And where on earth would
she go? When she tried to think ahead, weird fan-
cies crept into her mind and she was beset by a
number of nervous compulsions. It had come to the
point where she feared her own self as much as she
feared others. And all the time, unable to break
away, she had the feeling that some great disaster
was in wait for her.

'What's the matter, Alison?' Leonora asked. 'Are
you hungry? There's some sliced chicken in the icebox.' For the past few months Leonora often ad-
dressed Mrs. Langdon in a curious manner. She
worked her mouth exaggeratedly to form the
words and spoke in the careful and reasonable
voice that one would use when addressing an ab-
ject idiot. 'Both white meat and dark. *Very* good.
Mmmmh?'

'No, thank you.'

'Are you sure, darling?' the Major asked. 'You
don't want anything?'

'I'm quite all right. But would you mind—? Don't tap your heel like that on the floor. It bothers me.'

'I beg your pardon.'

The Major took his legs from under the table and crossed them sideways in his chair. On the surface the Major naïvely believed that his wife knew nothing about his affair. However, this soothing thought had become increasingly more difficult for him to hold on to; the strain of not realizing the truth had given him hemorrhoids and had almost upset his good digestion. He tried, and succeeded, in looking on her obvious unhappiness as something morbid and female, altogether outside his control. He remembered an incident that had happened soon after they were married. He had taken Alison out quail shooting and, although she had done target practice, she had never been hunting before. They had flushed a covey and he remembered still the pattern of the flying birds against the winter sunset. As he was watching Alison, he had only brought down one quail, and that one he insisted gallantly was hers. But when she took the bird from the dog's mouth, her face had changed. The bird was still living, so he brained it carelessly and then gave it back to her. She held the little warm, ruffled body that had somehow become degraded in its fall, and looked into the dead little glassy black eyes. Then she had burst into tears. That was the sort of thing the Major meant by 'fe-

male' and 'morbid'; and it did a man no good to try
to figure it all out. Also, when the Major was troubled about his wife these days he thought instinctively, as a means of self-defense, of a certain Lieutenant Weincheck, who was a company commander in the Major's own battalion and a close
friend of Alison's. So now as her face troubled his
conscience he said, to soothe himself:

'Did you say you spent the afternoon with Weincheck?'

'Yes, I was there,' she said.

'That's good. How did you find him?'

'Fairly well.' She decided suddenly to give the
sweater to Lieutenant Weincheck, as he could put
it to good use, and she hoped it was not too broad
across the shoulders.

'That man!' said Leonora. 'I can't understand
what in the world you see in him, Alison. Of
course I know you all get together and talk about
highbrow things. He calls me "Madam." He can't
stand me and he says "Yes, Madam," and "No,
Madam." Think of it!'

Mrs. Langdon smiled somewhat wryly, but made
no comment.

Here a few words might be due this Lieutenant
Weincheck, although with the exception of Mrs.
Langdon he was of no consequence to anyone on
the post. In the service he cut a sorry figure, as he
was nearing fifty and had never yet earned his
Captain's bars. His eyes gave him so much trouble

that soon he was to be retired. He lived in one of
the apartment houses set aside for bachelor lieutenants, most of whom were just out of West Point.
In his two small rooms was crowded an accumula-
tion of a lifetime, including a grand piano, a shelf
of phonograph albums, many hundreds of books, a
big Angora cat, and about a dozen potted plants.
He grew some sort of green creeper on the walls of
his sitting-room and often one was likely to stum-
ble over an empty beer bottle or a coffee cup that
had been set down on the floor. Finally, this old
Lieutenant played the violin. From his rooms there
would come the lost sound of some naked melody
from a string trio or quartet, a sound that made the
young officers passing along the corridor scratch
their heads and wink at each other. Here Mrs.
Langdon often came to visit in the late afternoon.
She and Lieutenant Weincheck would play Mozart
sonatas, or drink coffee and eat crystallized ginger
before the fire. In addition to his other handicaps
the Lieutenant was very poor, as he was trying to
send two nephews through school. He had to practice any number of mean little economies to make
ends meet, and his one dress uniform was so seedy
that he only attended the most obligatory social
affairs. When Mrs. Langdon learned that he did his
own mending, she got in the habit of bringing over
her own sewing and taking care of the Lieutenant's
underwear and linen along with her husband's.
Sometimes the two of them went in the Major's car

on trips together—to concerts in a city about a hundred and fifty miles away. On these occasions they took Anacleto with them.

'I'm putting up everything on this one hand and if I win I'll have every chip,' Mrs. Penderton said. 'It's about time we finished this.'

As Mrs. Penderton dealt, she managed to pick up an ace and king from her lap and give herself blackjack. Everyone in the room saw this and the Major chuckled. Also it was observed that the Major patted Leonora on her thigh underneath the table before he pushed back his chair. Mrs. Langdon got up at the same time and put her knitting in her bag.

'I must be getting along,' she said. 'But you stay, Morris, and don't break up the party. Good night everybody.'

Mrs. Langdon walked rather slowly and stiffly, and when she was gone Leonora said, 'I wonder what ails her now.'

'There's no telling,' said the Major miserably. 'But I guess I'll have to go. Here, let's make it one last round.'

Major Langdon hated to leave the cheerful room, but after he had told the Pendertons good-bye he stood for a time on the walk before the house. He was looking up at the stars and thinking that life sometimes was a bad business. He remembered suddenly the baby who had died. What bedlam all the way through! In her labor Alison had clung to Anacleto (for he, the Major, could not stand it) and she had screamed for thirty-three solid hours. And when the doctor said, 'You're not trying hard enough, bear down'—why, the little Filipino would bear down also, with bent knees and the sweat pouring down his face, giving out wail for wail with Alison. Then, when it was over, they found the baby's index and third fingers were grown together, and the Major's only thought was that if he had to touch that baby he would shudder all over.

It had drawn out for eleven months. They had been stationed in the Middle West and he would come in out of the snow to find something such as a cold plate of tuna fish salad in the icebox and the doctors and trained nurses all over the place. Anacleto would be upstairs bringing a diaper up to the light to judge the stool, or perhaps holding the baby for Alison while she walked up and down, up and down the room with her jaws clamped. When the whole business was over, he could feel nothing except relief. But not Alison! How bitter and cold it had left her! And how damned, damned finicky! Yes, life could be sad.

The Major opened the front door and saw Anacleto coming down the stairs. The little Filipino walked with grace and composure. He was dressed in sandals, soft gray trousers, and a blouse of aquamarine linen. His flat little face was creamy white and his black eyes glowed. He did not appear to notice the Major—but when he reached the bottom of the stairs he slowly raised his right leg, with the toes flexed like a ballet dancer's, and gave an airy little skip.

'Idiot!' the Major said. 'How is she?'

Anacleto lifted his eyebrows and closed his delicate white eyelids very slowly. '*Très fatiguée.*'

'Ah!' said the Major furiously, for he did not speak a word of French. 'Vooley voo rooney mooney mool I say, how is she?'

'*C'est les——*' But Anacleto himself had only recently taken up his study of French and he did not know of the word for 'sinuses.' However, he completed his reply with the most impressive dignity, '*Maître Corbeau sur un arbre perché,* Major.' He paused, snapped his fingers, and then added pensively, as though speaking aloud to himself, 'Some hot broth very attractively arranged.'

'You can fix me an Old Fashioned,' the Major said.

'I will suddenly,' said Anacleto. He knew very well that 'suddenly' could not be used in the place of 'immediately,' as he spoke choice and beautifully enunciated English in a voice that was exactly like Mrs. Langdon's; he made this mistake only in order further to addle the Major. 'I shall do so as soon as I have arranged the tray and made Madame Alison comfortable.'

By the Major's watch the preparations for this tray took thirty-eight minutes. The little Filipino aired about the kitchen in the liveliest manner and brought in a bowl of flowers from the dining-room. The Major watched him with his hairy fists on his hips. All the while Anacleto kept up a soft and vivacious chattering to himself. The Major caught something about Mr. Rudolph Serkin and about a cat which was walking around in a candy counter with bits of peanut-brittle stuck to its fur. In the meantime the Major mixed his own drink and fried himself two eggs. When this thirty-eight-minute tray was finished, Anacleto stood with his feet crossed, hands clasped behind his head, and rocked himself slowly.

'God! You're a rare bird,' the Major said. 'What I wouldn't do if I could get you in my battalion!'

The little Filipino shrugged. It was common knowledge that he thought the Lord had blundered grossly in the making of everyone except himself and Madame Alison—the sole exceptions to this were people behind footlights, midgets, great artists, and such-like fabulous folk. He looked down with satisfaction at the tray. On it were a cloth of yellow linen, a brown pottery jug of hot water, the broth cup, and two bouillon cubes. In the right corner there was a little blue Chinese rice bowl holding a bouquet of feathery Michaelmas daisies. Very deliberately Anacleto reached down, plucked off three of the blue petals, and placed them on the yellow napkin. He was not really as frisky as he appeared to be this evening. At times his eyes were anxious, and often he shot the Major a glance that was subtle, swift, and accusing.

'I'll take the tray up,' said the Major, for he saw that, although there was nothing to eat involved, it was the sort of thing that would please his wife and he might get the credit for it.

Alison sat propped in her bed with a book. In her reading glasses her face seemed all nose and eyes, and there were sickly blue shadows about the corners of her mouth. She wore a white linen nightgown and a bed-jacket of warm rose velvet. The room was very still and a fire burned on the hearth. There was little furniture, and the room, with its soft gray rug and cerise curtains, had a bare and very simple look. While Alison drank the broth, the Major, bored, sat in a chair by the bed and tried to think up something to say. Anacleto meddled lightly about the bed. He was whistling a melody that was sprightly, sad and clear.

'Look, Madame Alison!' he said suddenly. 'Do you feel well enough to discuss a certain matter with me?'

She put down her cup and took off her glasses. 'Why, what is it?'

'This!' Anacleto brought a footstool to the side of the bed and eagerly drew from his pocket some little scraps of cloth. 'These samples I ordered for us to look over. And now think back to the time two years ago when we passed by the window of Peck and Peck in New York City and I pointed out a certain little suit to you.' He selected one of the samples and handed it to her. 'This material made exactly in that way.'

'But I don't need a suit, Anacleto,' she said.

'Oh, but you do! You have not bought a garment in more than a year. And the green frock is *bien usée* at the elbows and ready for the Salvation Army.'

When Anacleto brought out his French phrase he gave the Major a glance of the merriest malice. It always made the Major feel rather eerie to listen to them talking together in the quiet room. Their voices and enunciation were so precisely alike that they seemed to be softly echoing each other. The only difference was that Anacleto spoke in a chattering, breathless manner, while Alison's voice was measured and composed.

'How much is it?' she asked.

'It is costly. But one could not expect to get such a quality for anything less. And think of the years of service.'

Alison turned back to her book again. 'We'll see about it.'

'For God's sake, go ahead and buy the dress,' the Major said. It bothered him to hear Alison haggle.

'And while we're about it we might order an extra yard so that I can have a jacket,' Anacleto said.

'All right. If I decide to get it.'

Anacleto poured Alison's medicine and made a

face for her as she drank it. Then he put an electric pad behind her back and brushed her hair. But as he started out of the room, he could not quite get past the full-length mirror on the closet door. He stopped and looked at himself, pointed his toe and cocked his head.

Then he turned back to Alison and began to whistle again. 'What is that? You and Lieutenant Weincheck were playing it last Thursday afternoon.'

'The opening bar of the Franck A Major Sonata.'

'Look!' said Anacleto excitedly. 'It has just this minute made me compose a ballet. Black velvet curtains and a glow like winter twilight. Very slowly, with the whole cast. Then a spotlight for the solo like a flame—very dashing, and with the waltz Mr. Sergei Rachmaninoff played. Then the finish goes back to the Franck, only this time——' He looked at Alison with his strange, bright eyes. 'Drunk!'

And with that he began to dance. He had been taken to the Russian ballet a year before and he had never got over it. Not a trick, not a gesture had escaped him. On the gray rug he moved about in a languid pantomime that slowed down until he stood quite still with his feet in their sandals crossed and his fingertips touched together in a meditative attitude. Then without warning he whirled lightly and began a furious little solo. It was apparent from his bright face that in his own

mind he was out on an immense stage, the cyno-
sure in a dazzling spectacle. Alison, also, was
plainly enjoying herself. The Major looked from
one to the other in disgusted disbelief. The last of
the dance was a drunken satire of the first. Anacleto finished with an odd little pose, his elbow
held in one hand and his fist to his chin with an
expression of wry puzzlement.

Alison burst out laughing. 'Bravo! Bravo! Anacleto!'

They laughed together and the little Filipino
leaned against the door, happy and a bit dazed. At
last he caught his breath and exclaimed in a mar-
veling voice, 'Have you ever noticed how well
"Bravo" and "Anacleto" go together?'

Alison stopped laughing and nodded thoughtfully. 'Indeed, Anacleto, I have noticed it many
times.'

The little Filipino hesitated in the doorway. He
glanced around the room to make sure that nothing
was wanting. Then he looked into her face and his
eyes were suddenly shrewd and very sad. 'Call me
if you need me,' he said shortly.

They heard him start down the stairs slowly,
then quicken to a skip. On the last steps he must
have tried something altogether too ambitious, for
there was a sudden thud. When the Major reached
the head of the stairs, Anacleto was picking himself
up with brave dignity.

'Did he hurt himself?' Alison asked tensely.

Anacleto looked up at the Major with angry tears in his eyes. 'I'm all right, Madame Alison,' he called.

The Major leaned forward and said slowly and soundlessly, working his mouth so that Anacleto could read the words, 'I—wish—you—had—bro—ken —your—neck.'

Anacleto smiled, shrugged his shoulders, and limped into the dining-room. When the Major went back to his wife, he found her reading. She did not look up at him, so he crossed the hall to his own room and slammed the door. His room was small, rather untidy, and the only ornaments in it were the cups he had won at horse shows. On the Major's bedside table there was an open book—a very recondite and literary book. The place was marked with a matchstick. The Major turned over forty pages or so, a reasonable evening's reading, and marked the new place with the match again. Then from under a pile of shirts in his bureau drawer he took a pulp magazine called *Scientifica-tion*. He settled himself comfortably in the bed and began reading of a wild, interplanetary superwar.

Across the hall from him, his wife had put down her book and was lying in a half-sitting position. Her face was stiff with pain and her dark, glittering eyes looked restlessly around the walls of the room. She was trying to make plans. She would divorce Morris, certainly. But how would she go about it? And above all how could she and Anacleto manage to make a living? She always had been contemptuous of women without children who accepted alimony, and her last shred of pride depended on the fact that she would not, could not, live on his money after she had left him. But what would they do—she and Anacleto? She had taught Latin in a girls' school the year before she married, but with her health as it was that would now be out of the question. A bookshop somewhere? It would have to be something that Anacleto could keep going when she was ill. Could the two of them possibly manage a prawn boat? Once she had talked to some shrimp fishermen on the coast. It had been a blue-and-gold seaside day and they had told her many things. She and Anacleto would stay out at sea all day with their nets lowered and there would be only the cold salt air, the ocean and the sun—Alison turned her head restlessly on the pillow. But what frippery!

It had been a shock, eight months ago, when she had learned about her husband. She and Lieutenant Weincheck and Anacleto had made a trip to the city with the intention of staying two days and nights for a concert and a play. But on the second day she was feverish and they decided to go back home. Late in the afternoon Anacleto had let her out at the front door and driven the car back to the garage. She had stopped on the front walk to look at some bulbs. It was almost dark and there was a light in her husband's room. The front door was locked and as she was standing there she saw Leonora's coat on the chest in the hall. And she had thought to herself how strange it was that if the Pendertons were there the front door should be locked. Then it occurred to her that they were mixing drinks in the kitchen while Morris had his bath. And she went around to the back. But then before she entered the house Anacleto rushed down the steps with such a horrified little face! He had whispered that they must go into town ten miles away as they had forgotten something. And when, rather dazed, she started up the steps he had caught her by the arm and said in a flat, frightened voice: 'You must not go in there now, Madame Alison.'

With what a shock it had come to her. She and Anacleto had got back into the car and driven off again. The insult of it happening in her own house—that was what she could not swallow. And then, of all times in the world, when they slowed down at the outpost there was a new soldier on duty who did not know them, and he had stopped the car. He looked into the little coupé as though they might be concealing a machine gun and then stood staring at Anacleto who, dressed in his jaunty burnt-orange jacket, was ready to burst into tears. He asked for the name in a tone of voice which suggested that he did not believe they could possibly screw up one between them.

Never would she forget that soldier's face. At the

moment she did not have it in her to speak her husband's name. The young soldier waited, stared, and said not a word. Later she had seen this same soldier at the stables when she went to fetch Morris in the car. He had the strange, rapt face of a Gauguin primitive. They looked at each other for perhaps a minute and at last an officer came up.

She and Anacleto had driven for three hours in the cold without speaking. And after that the plans she had made at night when she was sick and restless, schemes that as soon as the sun came up would seem so foolish. And the evening she had run home from the Pendertons' and done that ghastly thing. She had seen the garden shears on the wall and, beside herself with anger and despair, she had tried to stab and kill herself. But the shears were too blunt. And then for a few moments she must have been quite out of her head, for she herself did not know just how it had happened. Alison shuddered and hid her face in her hands. She heard her husband open his door and put his boots out in the hall. Quickly she turned off her light.

The Major had finished his magazine and hidden it again in the drawer. He took a last drink and then lay comfortably in the bed, looking up into the dark. What was it that meeting Leonora for the first time reminded him of? It had happened the year after the baby died, when for twelve solid months Alison had either been in the hospital or prowling around the house like a ghost. Then he had met Leonora down at the stables the first week he had come to this post, and she had offered to show him around. They left the bridle path and had a dandy gallop. When they had tied the horses for a rest, Leonora had seen some blackberry bushes near-by and said she might as well pick enough to make a cobbler for dinner. And Lord! when they were scrambling around those bushes together filling his hat with berries, it had first happened. At nine in the morning and two hours after they met! Even now he could hardly believe it. But what had it seemed like to him at the time? Oh, yes—it was like being out on maneuvers, shivering all through a cold rainy night in a tent that leaked. And then to get up at dawn and see that the rain was over and the sun was out again. And to watch the fine-looking soldiers making coffee over campfires and see the sparks rise up into a clear white sky. A wonderful feeling—the best in the world!

The Major giggled guiltily, hid his head underneath the sheet, and began to snore immediately.

At twelve-thirty Captain Penderton fretted alone in his study. He was working on a monograph and had made little progress that night. He had drunk a good deal of wine and tea and had smoked dozens of cigarettes. At last he had given up work altogether and now he was walking restlessly up and down the room. There are times when a man's greatest need is to have someone to love, some focal point for his diffused emotions. Also there are times when the irritations, disappointments, and fears of life, restless as spermatozoids, must be released in hate. The unhappy Captain had no one to hate and for the past months he had been miserable.

Alison Langdon, that big-nosed female Job, together with her loathsome Filipino—those two he abhorred. But he could not hate Alison, as she did not give him the opportunity. It chafed him no end to be under obligation to her. She was the only person in the world who knew of a certain woeful shortcoming in his nature; Captain Penderton was inclined to be a thief. He was continually resisting an urge to take things he saw in other people's houses. However, only twice had this weakness got the best of him. When he was a child of seven he had become so infatuated with the school-yard bully who had once beaten him that he stole from his aunt's dressing-table an old-fashioned hair-receiver as a love offering. And here on the post, twenty-seven years later, the Captain had once again succumbed.

At a dinner party given by a young bride he had been so fascinated by a certain piece of silver that he had carried it home in his pocket. It was an unusual and beautiful little dessert spoon, delicately chased and very old. The Captain had been miserably enchanted with it (the rest of the silver at his place was quite ordinary) and in the end he could not resist. When after some skillful manipulation he had his booty safe in his pocket, he realized that Alison, who was next to him, had seen the theft. She looked him full in the face with the most amazed expression. Even now he could not think of it without a shudder. And after a horribly long stare Alison had burst out laughing—yes, laughing. She laughed so hard that she choked herself and someone had to beat her on the back. Finally she excused herself from the table. And all through that tormenting evening whenever he looked at her she gave him such a mocking smile. Since then she was careful to keep a sharp watch on him when he was a guest at her table. The spoon was now hidden in his closet, wrapped carefully in a silk handkerchief and concealed in the box that his truss had come in.

But in spite of this he could not hate Alison. Nor could he truly hate his wife. Leonora maddened him to insanity, but even in the wildest fits of jealousy he could not hate her any more than he could hate a cat, or a horse, or a tiger cub. The Captain walked around in his study and once he gave the closed door a fretful kick. If that Alison finally made up her mind to divorce Morris, then how would it go? He could not bear to contemplate this possibility, so distressed was he at the thought of being left alone.

It seemed to the Captain that he heard a sound and he stopped short. The house was still. It has been mentioned before that the Captain was a coward. Sometimes when he was by himself he was overcome by a rootless terror. And now, as he stood in the silent room, it seemed that his nervousness and distress were not caused by forces within himself and others, things that in some measure he could control—but by some menacing outward circumstance which he could only sense from a distance. Fearfully the Captain looked all about the room. Then he straightened his desk and opened the door.

Leonora had fallen asleep on the rug before the fire in the sitting-room. The Captain looked down at her and laughed to himself. She was turned over on her side and he gave her a sharp little kick on the buttocks. She grumbled something about the stuffing for a turkey, but did not awake. The Captain bent down, shook her, talked into her face, and finally got her on her feet. But like a child who has to be aroused and taken to the toilet the last thing at night, Leonora had the gift of being able to remain asleep even while standing up. As the Captain led her ponderously to the stairs, her eyes were closed and she still grumbled about the turkey.

'I'll be damned if I'll undress you,' the Captain said.

But Leonora sat where he had left her on the bed, and after watching her for several minutes he laughed again and took off her clothes. He did not put a nightgown on her, for the bureau drawers were in such a mess he could not find one. Besides, Leonora always liked sleeping 'in the raw,' as she called it. When she was in bed, the Captain went up to a picture on the wall that had amused him for years. It was a photograph of a girl of about seventeen, and at the bottom there was written the touching inscription: 'To Leonora with Oodles of Love from Bootsie.' This masterpiece had adorned the walls of Leonora's bedrooms for more than a decade, and had been carried halfway around the globe. But when questioned about Bootsie, who for a time had been her roommate in a boarding-school, Leonora said vaguely that it seemed to her that she had once heard Bootsie had drowned some years ago. Indeed, after pressing her about this matter, he found she did not even remember this Bootsie's lawful name. And yet, simply because of habit, the picture had hung on her wall for eleven years. The Captain looked once again at his wife as she lay sleeping. She was hot-natured and already the cover had been pushed down below her naked breasts. She smiled in her sleep, and it occurred to the Captain that she was now eating the turkey she had prepared in her dream.

The Captain used Seconal, and his habit was of such long standing that one capsule had no effect on him. He considered that with his hard work at the Infantry School it was a great imposition for him to have to lie awake at night and get up jaded the next morning. Without sufficient Seconal his slumber was light and wrought with dreams. Tonight he decided to treat himself to a triple dose, and he knew that then he would drop immediately into a blunt, sodden sleep that would last six or seven hours. The Captain swallowed his capsules and lay down in the dark with pleasant anticipation. This quantity of the drug gave him a unique and voluptuous sensation; it was as though a great dark bird alighted on his chest, looked at him once with fierce, golden eyes, and stealthily enfolded him in his dark wings.

Private Williams waited outside the house until the lights had been out for almost two hours. The stars were faded a little and the blackness of the night sky had changed to a deep violet. Still, however, Orion was brilliant and the Big Dipper shone with a wonderful radiance. The soldier walked around to the back of the house and quietly tried the screen door. It was fastened from the inside, as he knew it would be. However, the door was slightly loose and when the soldier inserted the blade of his knife in the crack he was able to raise the hook latch. The back door itself was not locked.

Once inside the house the soldier waited for a moment. All was dark and there was not a sound. He stared about him with his wide, vague eyes until he was accustomed to the darkness. The plan of the house was already familiar to him. The long

front hall and the stairs divided the house, leaving
on one side the large sitting-room and, farther
back, the servant's room. On the other side were
the dining-room, the Captain's study, and the
kitchen. Upstairs to the right there was a double
bedroom and a small cubicle. To the left were two
bedrooms of medium size. The Captain used the
large room and his wife slept across the hall from
him. The soldier walked carefully up the stairs,
which were carpeted. He moved with deliberate
composure. The door of The Lady's room was
open, and when he reached it the soldier did not
hesitate. With the lithe silence of a cat he stepped
inside.

Green shadowy moonlight filled the room. The
Captain's wife slept as her husband had left her.
Her soft hair lay loosened upon the pillow and her
gently breathing chest was half-uncovered. A yellow silk spread was on the bed and an open flask
of perfume sweetened the air with a drowsy scent.
Very slowly the soldier tiptoed to the side of the
bed and bent over the Captain's wife. The moon
softly lighted their faces and he was so close that
he could feel her warm, even breath. In the soldier's grave eyes there was at first an expression of
intent curiosity, but as the moments passed a look
of bliss awakened in his heavy face. The young soldier felt in him a keen, strange sweetness that
never before in his life had he known.

He stood in this way, bent close over the Captain's wife, for some time. Then he touched his hand to the window-sill to steady himself and very slowly squatted down beside the bed. He balanced himself on the broad balls of his feet, his back held straight, and his strong delicate hands resting on his knees. His eyes were round as amber buttons and his bangs lay in a tangled mat on his forehead.

On a few occasions before this Private Williams had had this look of suddenly awakened happiness in his face, but no one on the post had seen him then. If he had been seen at such a time he would have been court-martialed. The truth was that in his long ramblings through the forest of the reservation the soldier was sometimes not alone. When he could get leave from work in the afternoon, he took a certain horse from the stables with him. He rode about five miles from the post to a secluded spot, far from any paths, that was difficult to reach. Here in the woods there was a flat, clear space, covered with a grassy weed of the color of burnished bronze. In this lonely place the soldier always unsaddled his horse and let him go free. Then he took off his clothes and lay down on a large flat rock in the middle of the field. For there was one thing that this soldier could not do without—the sun. Even on the coldest days he would lie still and naked and let the sunlight soak into his flesh. Sometimes, still naked, he stood on the rock and slipped upon the horse's bare back. His horse was an ordinary army plug which, with anyone but

Private Williams, could sustain only two gaits—a clumsy trot and a rocking-horse gallop. But with the soldier a marvelous change came over the animal; he cantered or single-footed with proud, stiff elegance. The soldier's body was of a pale golden brown and he held himself erect. Without his clothes he was so slim that the pure, curved outlines of his ribs could be seen. As he cantered about in the sunlight, there was a sensual, savage smile on his lips that would have surprised his barrack mates. After such outings he came back weary to the stables and spoke to no one.

Private Williams squatted by the bed in The Lady's room until almost dawn. He did not move, or make a sound, or take his eyes from the body of the Captain's wife. Then, as the day was breaking, he balanced himself again with his hand on the window-sill and got up carefully. He went down the stairs and closed the back door cautiously behind him. Already the sky was a pale blue and Venus was fading.

iii

Alison Langdon had lived through a night of torment. She did not sleep until the sun came up and the bugle sounded reveille. During those long hours many eerie thoughts had troubled her. Once just at dawn she even fancied, she was almost sure, that she saw someone come out of the Pendertons' house and walk off into the woods. Then, soon after she finally got to sleep, a great racket awakened her. Hurriedly she put on her bathrobe, went downstairs, and found herself confronting a shock-

ing and ridiculous spectacle. Her husband was
chasing Anacleto round and round the dining-room
table with a boot in his hand. He was in his sock
feet, but otherwise completely uniformed for Saturday morning inspection. His sword banged against
his thigh as he ran. They both stopped short when
they saw her. Then Anacleto hastened to take ref-
uge behind her back.

'He did it on purpose!' the Major said in an out-
raged voice. 'I'm already late. Six hundred men are
waiting for me. And look, just please take a glance,
at what he brings me!'

The boots indeed were a sorry sight. It looked as
though they had been rubbed over with flour and
water. She scolded Anacleto and stood over him as
he cleaned them properly. He wept piteously, but
she found the strength of mind not to console him.
When he had finished, Anacleto mentioned something about running away from home and opening
a linen shop in Quebec. She carried the polished
boots up to her husband and handed them to him
without a word, but with a look that took care of
him also. Then, as her heart bothered her, she went
back to bed with her book.

Anacleto brought her up her coffee and then
drove over to the Post Exchange to do the market-
ing for Sunday. Later in the morning, when she
had finished her book and was looking out the window at the sunny autumn day, he came to her
room again. He was blithe, and had quite forgotten

the scolding about the boots. He built up a roaring
fire and then quietly opened the top bureau
drawer to do a bit of meddling. He took out a little
crystal cigarette lighter which she had had made
from an old-fashioned vinaigrette. This trinket so
fascinated him that she had given it to him years
ago. He still kept it with her things, however, so
that he would have a legitimate reason for opening
the drawer whenever he wished. He asked for the
loan of her glasses and peered for a long time at
the linen scarf on the chest of drawers. Then with
his thumb and forefinger he picked up something
invisible and carefully carried this speck over to
the wastebasket. He was talking away to himself,
but she paid no attention to his chatter.

What would become of Anacleto when she was
dead? That was a question that worried her constantly. Morris, of course, had promised her never
to let him be in want—but what would such a
promise be worth when Morris married again, as
he would be sure to do? She remembered the time
seven years ago in the Philippines when Anacleto
first came to her household. What a sad, strange
little creature he had been! He was so tormented
by the other houseboys that he dogged her footsteps all day long. If anyone so much as looked at
him he would burst into tears and wring his hands.
He was seventeen years old, but his sickly, clever,
frightened face had the innocent expression of a
child of ten. When they were making preparations

to return to the States, he had begged her to take him with her, and she had done so. The two of them, she and Anacleto, could perhaps find a way to get along in the world together—but what would he do when she was gone?

'Anacleto, are you happy?' she asked him suddenly.

The little Filipino was not one to be disturbed by any unexpected, intimate question. 'Why, certainly,' he said, without a moment's consideration. 'When you are well.'

The sun and firelight were bright in the room. There was a dancing spectrum on one of the walls and she watched this, half-listening to Anacleto's soft conversation. 'What I find it so difficult to realize is that they *know*,' he was saying. Often he would begin a discussion with such a vague and mysterious remark, and she waited to catch the drift of it later. 'It was not until after I had been in your service for a long time that I really believed that you knew. Now I can believe it about everybody else except Mr. Sergei Rachmaninoff.'

She turned her face toward him. 'What are you talking about?'

'Madame Alison,' he said, 'do you yourself really believe that Mr. Sergei Rachmaninoff knows that a chair is something to be sat on and that a clock shows one the time? And if I should take off my shoe and hold it up to his face and say, "What is this, Mr. Sergei Rachmaninoff?" then he would answer, like anyone else, "Why, Anacleto, that is a shoe." I myself find it hard to realize.'

The Rachmaninoff recital had been the last concert they had heard, and consequently from Anacleto's point of view it was the best. She herself did not care for crowded concert halls and would have preferred to spend the money on phonograph records—but it was good to get away from the post occasionally, and these trips were the joy of Anacleto's life. For one thing they stayed the night in a hotel, which was an enormous delight to him.

'Do you think if I beat your pillows you would be more comfortable?' Anacleto asked.

And the dinner the night of that last concert! Anacleto sailed proudly after her into the hotel dining-room wearing his orange velvet jacket. When it was his turn to order, he held the menu up to his face and then completely closed his eyes. To the astonishment of the colored waiter he ordered in French. And although she had wanted to burst out laughing, she controlled herself and translated after him with the best gravity she could assume—as though she were a sort of duenna or lady-in-waiting to him. Because of his limited French this dinner of his was rather peculiar. He had got it out of the lesson in his book called 'Le Jardin Potager,' and his order consisted only of cabbage, string beans, and carrots. So when on her own she had added an order of chicken for him, Anacleto had opened his eyes just long enough to give her a deep, grateful little look. The white-coated waiters clustered about this phenomenon like flies, and Anacleto was much too exalted to touch a crumb.

'Suppose we have some music,' she said. 'Let's hear the Brahms G Minor Quartet.'

'*Fameux*,' said Anacleto.

He put on the first record and settled down to listen on his footstool by the fire. But the opening passage, the lovely dialogue between the piano and the strings, was hardly completed when there was a knock on the door. Anacleto spoke to someone in the hall, closed the door again, and turned off the phonograph.

'Mrs. Penderton,' he whispered, lifting his eyebrows.

'I knew I could knock on the door downstairs till doomsday and you all would never hear me with this music going on,' Leonora said when she came into the room. She sat down on the foot of the bed so hard that it felt as though she had broken a spring. Then, remembering that Alison was not well, Leonora tried to look sickly also, as that was her notion of the proper behavior in a sickroom. 'Do you think you can make it tonight?'

'Make what?'

'Why, my God, Alison! My party! I've been working like a nigger for the past three days getting everything ready. I don't give a party like this but twice a year.'

'Of course,' said Alison. 'It just slipped my mind for a moment.'

'Listen!' said Leonora, and her fresh rosy face flamed suddenly with anticipation. 'I just wish you could see my kitchen now. Here's the way it will go. I'm putting in all the leaves in the dining-room table and everybody will just mill around and help themselves. I'm having a couple of Virginia hams, a huge turkey, fried chicken, sliced cold pork, plenty of barbecued spareribs, and all sorts of little knickknacks like pickled onions and olives and radishes. And hot rolls and little cheese biscuits passed around. The punchbowl is in the corner, and for people who like their liquor straight I'm having on the sideboard eight quarts of Kentucky Bourbon, five of rye, and five of Scotch. And an entertainer from town is coming out to play the accordion——'

'But who on earth is going to eat all that food?' Alison asked, with a little swallow of nausea.

'The whole shebang,' said Leonora enthusiastically. 'I've telephoned everybody from Old Sugar's wife on down.'

'Old Sugar' was Leonora's name for the Commanding General of the post, and she called him by it to his face. With the General, as with all men, she had a flip and affectionate manner, and the General, like most of the officers on the post, fairly ate out of her hand. The General's wife was very fat, slow, gushed over, and completely out of things.

'One thing I came over about this morning,' said Leonora, 'is to find out if Anacleto will serve the punch for me.'

'He will be glad to help you out,' Alison answered for him.

Anacleto, who was standing in the doorway, did not look so glad about it. He glanced reproachfully at Alison and went downstairs to see about luncheon.

'Susie's two brothers are helping in the kitchen and, my God, how that crowd can eat! I never saw anything to equal it. We——'

'By the way,' said Alison, 'is Susie married?'

'Heavens, no! She won't have anything to do with men. She got caught when she was fourteen years old and has never forgotten it. But why?'

'I just wondered because I was almost sure that I saw someone go into your house by the back way late last night and come out again before dawn.'

'You just imagined it,' said Leonora soothingly. She considered Alison to be quite off her head, and did not believe even the simplest remark that she made.

'Perhaps so.'

Leonora was bored and ready to go home. Still, she thought that a neighborly visit should last at least an hour, so she stuck it out dutifully. She sighed and tried again to look somewhat ill. It was her idea, when she was not too carried away with thoughts of food and sport, that the tactful topic of conversation in a sickroom was an account of other illnesses. Like all very stupid people she had a predilection for the gruesome, which she could indulge in or throw off at will. Her repertoire of tragedies was limited for the most part to violent sporting accidents.

'Did I tell you about the thirteen-year-old girl who came along with us on a fox hunt as a whipper-in and broke her neck?'

'Yes, Leonora,' said Alison in a voice of controlled exasperation. 'You have told me of every terrible detail five times.'

'Does it make you nervous?'

'Extremely.'

'Hmmm——' said Leonora. She was not at all troubled by this rebuff. Calmly she lighted a cigarette. 'Don't ever let anybody tell you that's the way to fox-hunt. I know. I've hunted both ways. Listen, Alison!' She worked her mouth exaggeratedly and spoke in a deliberately encouraging voice as though addressing a small child. 'Do you know how to hunt 'possums?'

Alison nodded shortly and straightened the counterpane. 'You tree them.'

'On foot,' said Leonora. 'That's the way to hunt a fox. Now this uncle of mine has a cabin in the mountains and my brothers and I used to visit him. About six of us would start out with our dogs on a cold evening when the sun had set. A colored boy would run along behind with a jug of good mellow corn on his back. Sometimes we'd be after a fox all night long in the mountains. Gosh, I can't tell you about it. Somehow——' The feeling was in Leonora, but she had not the words to express it.

'Then to have one last drink at six o'clock and sit down to breakfast. And, God! everybody said this uncle of mine was peculiar, but he sure set a good table. After a hunt we'd come in to a table just loaded with fish roe, broiled ham, fried chicken, biscuits the size of your hand——'

When Leonora was gone at last, Alison did not know whether to laugh or cry; she did a little of both, rather hysterically. Anacleto came up to her and carefully beat out the big dent at the foot of the bed where Leonora had been sitting.

'I am going to divorce the Major, Anacleto,' she said suddenly when she had stopped laughing. 'I will inform him of it tonight.'

From Anacleto's expression she could not tell whether or not this was a surprise to him. He waited for a time and then asked: 'Then where shall we go after that, Madame Alison?'

Through her mind passed a long panorama of plans which she had made during sleepless nights—tutoring Latin in some college town, shrimp fishing, hiring Anacleto out to drudge while she sat in a boarding-house and took in sewing—— But she only said: 'That I have not yet decided.'

'I wonder,' Anacleto said meditatively, 'what the Pendertons will do about it.'

'You needn't wonder because that is not our affair.'

Anacleto's little face was dark and thoughtful. He stood with his hands resting on the footpiece of the bed. She felt that he had some further question to put to her, and she looked up at him and waited. Finally he asked hopefully, 'Do you think we might live in a hotel?'

In the afternoon Captain Penderton went down to the stables for his usual ride. Private Williams was still on duty, although he was to be free that day at four o'clock. When the Captain spoke, he did not look at the young soldier and his voice was high-pitched and arrogant.

'Saddle Mrs. Penderton's horse, Firebird.'

Private Williams stood motionless, staring into the Captain's white, strained face. 'The Captain said?'

'Firebird,' the Captain repeated. 'Mrs. Penderton's horse.'

This order was unusual; Captain Penderton had ridden Firebird only three times before, and on each of these occasions his wife had been with him. The Captain himself did not own a horse, and used the mounts belonging to the stable. As he waited out in the open court, the Captain nervously jerked the fingertips of his glove. Then, when Firebird was led out, he was not satisfied; Private Williams had put on Mrs. Penderton's flat, English type saddle, while the Captain preferred an army

McClellan. As this change was being made, the Captain looked into the horse's round, purple eyes and saw there a liquid image of his own frightened face. Private Williams held the bridle as he mounted. The Captain sat tense, his jaws hard, and his knees gripping the saddle desperately. The soldier still stood impassive with his hand on the bridle.

After a moment the Captain said:

'Well, Private, you can see that I am seated. Let go!'

Private Williams stepped back a few paces. The Captain held tight to the reins and hardened his thighs. Nothing happened. The horse did not plunge and strain at the bit as he did each morning with Mrs. Penderton, but waited quietly for the signal to start. When the Captain realized this, he quickened with a sudden vicious joy. 'Ah,' he thought. 'She has broken his spirit as I knew she would.' The Captain dug in his heels and struck the horse with his short, plaited crop. They started on the bridle path at a gallop.

The afternoon was fine and sunny. The air was bracing, bitter sweet with the odor of pines and rotting leaves. Not a cloud could be seen in all the wide blue sky. The horse, which had not been exercised that day, seemed to go a little mad from the pleasure of galloping with unchecked freedom. Firebird, like most horses, was apt to be hard to manage if given free rein immediately after being led out from the pasture. The Captain knew this; therefore his next action was a very curious one. They had galloped rhythmically for perhaps three quarters of a mile when suddenly, with no preliminary tightening of the reins, the Captain jerked the horse up short. He pulled the reins with such unexpected sharpness that Firebird lost his balance, sidestepped awkwardly and reared. Then he stood quite still, surprised but tractable. The Captain was exceedingly satisfied.

This procedure was repeated twice. The Captain gave Firebird his head just long enough for the joy of freedom to be aroused and then checked him without warning. This sort of behavior was not new to the Captain. Often in his life he had exacted many strange and secret little penances on himself which he would have found difficult to explain to others.

The third time the horse stopped as usual, but at this point something happened which disturbed the Captain so that all of his satisfaction instantly vanished. As they were standing still, alone on the path, the horse slowly turned his head and looked into the Captain's face. Then deliberately he lowered his head to the ground with his ears flattened back.

The Captain felt suddenly that he was to be thrown, and not only thrown but killed. The Captain always had been afraid of horses: he only rode because it was the thing to do, and because this

was another one of his ways of tormenting himself.
He had had his wife's comfortable saddle ex-
changed for the clumsy McClellan for the reason
that the raised saddlebow gave him something to
grasp in case of an emergency. Now he sat rigid,
trying to hold to the saddle and the reins at the
same time. Then, so great was his sudden appre-
hension, he gave up completely in advance, slipped
his feet from the stirrups, lifted his hands to his
face, and looked about him to see where he would
fall. This weakness lasted only a few moments,
however. When the Captain realized that he was
not to be thrown after all, a great feeling of
triumph came in him. They started at a gallop
once more.

The path had been leading steadily upward with
the woods on either side. Now they approached
the bluff from which could be seen miles of the reservation. Far in the distance the green pine forest
made a dark line against the bright autumn sky.
Struck by the wonder of the view, the Captain had
it in his mind to pause for a moment and he drew
in his reins. But here a totally unexpected happening occurred, an incident that might have cost the
Captain his life. They were still riding hard when
they reached the top of the ridge. At this point,
without warning and with the speed of a demon,
the horse swerved to the left and plunged down
the side of the embankment.

The Captain was so stunned that he lost his seat.

He was hurled forward on the horse's neck and his feet dangled stirrupless. Somehow he managed to hold on. With one hand grasping the mane and the other feebly holding to the reins, he was able to slide himself back into the saddle. But that was all he could do. They were riding with such dizzying speed that his head swam when he opened his eyes. He could not find his seat firmly enough to control the reins. And he knew in one fateful instant that even so it would be of no use; there was not the power in him to stop this horse. Every muscle, every nerve in his body was intent on only one purpose—to hold on. With the speed of Firebird's great racing sire they were flying over the wide open space of sward that separated the bluff from the woods. The grass was glinted with bronze and red beneath the sun. Then suddenly the Captain felt a green dimness fall over them and he knew that they had entered the forest by way of some narrow footpath. Even when the horse had left the open space, he seemed hardly to slacken his speed. The dazed Captain was in half-crouching position. A thorn from a tree ripped open his left cheek. The Captain felt no pain, but he saw vividly the hot scarlet blood that dripped on his arm. He crouched down so that the right side of his face rubbed against the short stiff hair of Firebird's neck. Clinging desperately to the mane, the reins, and the saddlebow, he dared not raise his head for fear it would be broken by the branch of a tree.

Three words were in the Captain's heart. He shaped them soundlessly with his trembling lips, as he had not breath to spare for a whisper: 'I am lost.'

And having given up life, the Captain suddenly began to live. A great mad joy surged through him. This emotion, coming as unexpectedly as the plunge of the horse when he had broken away, was one that the Captain had never experienced. His eyes were glassy and half-open, as in delirium, but he saw suddenly as he had never seen before. The world was a kaleidoscope, and each of the multiple visions which he saw impressed itself on his mind with burning vividness. On the ground half-buried in the leaves there was a little flower, dazzling white and beautifully wrought. A thorny pine cone, the flight of a bird in the blue windy sky, a fiery shaft of sunshine in the green gloom—these the Captain saw as though for the first time in his life. He was conscious of the pure keen air and he felt the marvel of his own tense body, his laboring heart, and the miracle of blood, muscle, nerves, and bone. The Captain knew no terror now; he had soared to that rare level of consciousness where the mystic feels that the earth is he and that he is the earth. Clinging crabwise to the runaway horse, there was a grin of rapture on his bloody mouth.

How long this mad ride lasted the Captain would never know. Toward the end he knew that they had come out from the woods and were galloping through an open plain. It seemed to him that from the corner of his eye he saw a man lying on a rock in the sun and a horse grazing. This did not surprise him and in an instant was forgotten. The only thing which concerned the Captain now was the fact that when they entered the forest again the horse was giving out. In an agony of dread the Captain thought: 'When this ends, all will be over for me.'

The horse slowed to an exhausted trot and at last stopped altogether. The Captain raised himself in the saddle and looked about him. When he struck the horse in the face with the reins, they stumbled on a few paces farther. Then the Captain could make him go no farther. Trembling, he dismounted. Slowly and methodically he tied the horse to a tree. He broke off a long switch, and with the last of his spent strength he began to beat the horse savagely. Breathing in great gasps, his coat dark and curled with sweat, the horse at first moved restively about the tree. The Captain kept on beating him. Then at last the horse stood motionless and gave a broken sigh. A pool of sweat darkened the pine straw beneath him and his head hung down. The Captain threw the whip away. He was smeared with blood, and a rash caused by rubbing against the horse's bristly hair had come out on his face and neck. His anger was unappeased and he could hardly stand from exhaustion. He sank down on the ground and lay in a curious position with his head in his arms. Out in the forest there, the Captain looked like a broken doll that has been thrown away. He was sobbing aloud.

For a brief time the Captain lost consciousness. Then, as he came out of his faint, he had a vision of the past. He looked back at the years behind him as one stares at a shaking image at the bottom of a well. He remembered his boyhood. He had been brought up by five old-maid aunts. His aunts were not bitter except when alone; they laughed a great deal and were constantly arranging picnics, fussy excursions, and Sunday dinners to which they invited other old maids. Nevertheless, they had used the little boy as a sort of fulcrum to lift the weight of their own heavy crosses. The Captain had never known real love. His aunts gushed over him with sentimental effulgence and knowing no better he repaid them with the same counterfeit coin. In addition, the Captain was a Southerner and was never allowed by his aunts to forget it. On his mother's side he was descended from Huguenots who left France in the seventeenth century, lived in Haiti until the great uprising, and then were planters in Georgia before the Civil War. Behind him was a history of barbarous splendor, ruined poverty, and family hauteur. But the present generation had not come to much; the Captain's only male first cousin was a policeman in the city of Nashville. Being a great snob, and with no real pride in him, the Captain set exaggerated store by the lost past.

The Captain kicked his feet on the pine straw and sobbed with a high wail that echoed thinly in the woods. Then abruptly he lay still and quiet. A strange feeling that had lingered in him for some time took sudden shape. He was sure that there was someone near him. Painfully he turned himself over on his back.

At first the Captain did not believe what he saw. Two yards from him, leaning against an oak tree, the young soldier whose face the Captain hated looked down at him. He was completely naked. His slim body glistened in the late sun. He stared at the Captain with vague, impersonal eyes as though looking at some insect he had never seen before. The Captain was too paralyzed by surprise to move. He tried to speak, but only a dry rattle came from his throat. As he watched him, the soldier turned his gaze to the horse. Firebird was still soaked with sweat and there were welts on his rump. In one afternoon the horse seemed to have changed from a thoroughbred to a plug fit for the plow.

The Captain lay between the soldier and the horse. The naked man did not bother to walk around his outstretched body. He left his place by the tree and lightly stepped over the officer. The Captain had a close swift view of the young soldier's bare foot; it was slim and delicately built, with a high instep marked by blue veins. The soldier untied the horse and put his hand to his muzzle in a caressing gesture. Then, without a glance at the Captain, he led the horse off into the dense woods.

It had happened so quickly that the Captain had not found a chance to sit up or to utter a word. At first he could feel only astonishment. He dwelt on the pure-cut lines of the young man's body. He called out something inarticulate and received no reply. A rage came in him. He felt a rush of hatred for the soldier that was as exorbitant as the joy he had experienced on runaway Firebird. All the humiliations, the envies, and the fears of his life found vent in this great anger. The Captain stumbled to his feet and started blindly through the darkening woods.

He did not know where he was, or how far he had come from the post. His mind swarmed with a dozen cunning schemes by which he could make the soldier suffer. In his heart the Captain knew that this hatred, passionate as love, would be with him all the remaining days of his life.

After walking for a long time, when it was almost night, he found himself on a path familiar to him.

The Pendertons' party began at seven, and half an hour later the front rooms were crowded. Leonora, stately in a gown of cream-colored velvet, re-

ceived her guests alone. When replying to inquiries
about the absence of the host, she said that, devil
take him, she didn't know—he might have run
away from home. Everyone laughed and repeated
this—they pictured the Captain trudging off with a
stick over his shoulder and his notebooks wrapped
in a red bandanna. He had planned to drive into
town after his ride and perhaps he was having car
trouble.

The long table in the dining-room was more
than lavishly laid and replenished. The air was so
thick with the odors of ham, spareribs, and whiskey that it seemed one might almost eat it with a
spoon. From the sitting-room came the sound of
the accordion, augmented from time to time by
bits of spurious part singing. The sideboard was
perhaps the gayest spot. Anacleto, with an im-
posed-on expression, ladled stingy half-cups of
punch and took his time about it. After he spotted
Lieutenant Weincheck, standing alone near the
front door, he was engaged for fifteen minutes in
fishing out every cherry and piece of pineapple,
then he left a dozen officers waiting in order to
present this choice cup to the old Lieutenant.
There was so much lively conversation that it was
impossible to follow any one line of thought. There
was talk of the new army appropriation by the
Government and gossip about a recent suicide.
Below the general hubbub, and with cautious
glances to ascertain the whereabouts of Major

Langdon, a joke sneaked its way through the party—a story to the effect that the little Filipino thoughtfully scented Alison Langdon's specimen of wee-wee with perfume before taking it to the hospital for a urinalysis. The congestion was beginning to be disastrous. Already a tart had fallen from a plate and, unnoticed, had been tracked halfway up the stairs.

Leonora was in the highest spirits. She had a gay cliché for everyone, and she patted the Quartermaster Colonel, an old favorite of hers, on top of his bald head. Once she left the hall personally to carry a drink to the young entertainer from town who played the accordion. 'My God! the talent this boy has!' she said. 'Why, he can play anything at all you hum to him! "Oh Pretty Red Wing"—anything!'

'Really wonderful,' Major Langdon agreed, and looked at the group clustered around. 'Now my wife goes in for classical stuff—Bach, you know—all that. But to me it's like swallowing a bunch of angleworms. Now take "The Merry Widows' Waltz"—that's the sort of thing I love. Tuneful music!'

The gliding waltz, together with the arrival of the General, quieted some of the racket. Leonora was enjoying her party so much that it was not until after eight o'clock that she began to be concerned about her husband. Already most of the guests were bewildered by the protracted absence of their host. There was even the lively feeling that some accident might have occurred, or that an unexpected scandal was afoot. Consequently, even the earliest arrivals tended to stay on long past the customary time for such a coming-and-going affair; the house was so crowded that it took a keen sense of strategy to get from one room to the next.

Meanwhile, Captain Penderton waited at the entrance of the bridle path with a hurricane lamp and the Sergeant in charge of the stables. He had reached the post well after dark and his story was that the horse had thrown him and run away. They were hoping that Firebird would find his way back. The Captain had bathed his wounded, rash-red face, and then had driven to the hospital and had three stitches put in his cheek. But he could not go home. Not only did he lack the daring to face Leonora until the horse was in his stall—the real reason was that he was in wait for the man he hated. The night was mild, bright, and the moon was in its third quarter.

At nine o'clock they heard in the distance the sound of horses' hoofs, coming in very slowly. Soon the weary, shadowy figures of Private Williams and the two horses could be seen. The soldier led them both by the bridle. Blinking a little, he came up to the hurricane lamp. He looked into the Captain's face with such a long strange stare that the Sergeant felt a sudden shock. He did not know what to make of this, and he left it with the Captain to deal with the situation. The Captain was silent, but his eyelids twitched and his hard mouth trembled.

The Captain followed Private Williams into the stable. The young soldier fed the horses mash and gave them a rubdown. He did not speak, and the Captain stood outside the stall and watched him. He looked at the fine, skillful hands and the tender roundness of the soldier's neck. The Captain was overcome by a feeling that both repelled and fascinated him—it was as though he and the young soldier were wrestling together naked, body to body, in a fight to death. The Captain's strained loin muscles were so weak that he could hardly stand. His eyes, beneath his twitching eyelids, were like blue burning flames. The soldier quietly finished his work and left the stable. The Captain followed and stood watching as he walked off into the night. They had not spoken a word.

It was only when he got into his automobile that the Captain remembered the party at his house.

Anacleto did not come home until late in the evening. He stood in the doorway of Alison's room looking rather green and jaded, as crowds exhausted him. 'Ah,' he said philosophically, 'the world is choked up with too many people.'

Alison saw, however, from a swift little snap of his eyes, that something had happened. He went into her bathroom and rolled up the sleeves of his yellow linen shirt to wash his hands. 'Did Lieutenant Weincheck come over to see you?'

'Yes, he visited with me quite a while.'

The Lieutenant had been depressed. She sent him downstairs for a bottle of sherry. Then after they had drunk the wine he sat by the bed with the chessboard on his knees and they played a game of Russian bank. She had not realized until too late that it was very tactless of her to suggest the game, as the Lieutenant could hardly make out the cards and tried to hide this failing from her.

'He has just heard that the medical board did not pass him,' she said. 'He will get his retirement papers shortly.'

'Tsskl What a pity!' Then Anacleto added, 'At the same time I should be glad about it if I were he.'

The doctor had left her a new prescription that afternoon and from the bathroom mirror she saw Anacleto examine the bottle carefully and then take a taste of it before measuring it out for her. Judging by the look on his face, he did not much like the flavor. But he smiled brightly when he came back into the room.

'You have never been to such a party,' he said. 'What a great constellation!'

'Consternation, Anacleto.'

'At any rate, havoc. Captain Penderton was two hours late to his own party. Then, when he came in, I thought he had been half-eaten by a lion. The

horse threw him in a blackberry bush and ran
away. You have never seen such a face.'

'Did he break any bones?'

'He looked to me as though he had broken his
back,' said Anacleto, with some satisfaction. 'But he
carried it off fairly well—went upstairs and put on
his evening clothes and tried to pretend that he
wasn't upset. Now everybody has left except the
Major and the Colonel with the red hair whose
wife looks like a woery woman.'

'Anacleto,' she warned him softly. Anacleto had
used the term 'woery woman' several times before
she caught on to the meaning. At first she had
thought it might be a native term, and then it had
come to her finally that he meant 'whore.'

Anacleto shrugged his shoulders and then turned
suddenly to her, his face flushed. 'I hate people!' he
said vehemently. 'At the party someone told this
joke, not knowing that I was near. And it was vul-
gar and insulting and not true!'

'What do you mean?'

'I wouldn't repeat it to you.'

'Well, forget it,' she said. 'Go on to bed and have
a good night's sleep.'

Alison was troubled over Anacleto's outburst. It
seemed to her that she also loathed people. Everyone she had known in the past five years was somehow wrong—that is, everyone except Weincheck
and of course Anacleto and little Catherine. Morris
Langdon in his blunt way was as stupid and heart-

less as a man could be. Leonora was nothing but an animal. And thieving Weldon Penderton was at bottom hopelessly corrupt. What a gang! Even she herself she loathed. If it were not for sordid procrastination and if she had a rag of pride, she and Anacleto would not be in this house tonight.

She turned her face to the window and looked into the night. A wind had come up, and downstairs a loose shutter was banging against the side of the house. She turned off the light so that she could see out of the window. Orion was wonderfully clear and bright tonight. In the forest the tops of the trees moved in the wind like dark waves. It was then that she glanced down toward the Pendertons' house and saw a man standing again by the edge of the woods. The man himself was hidden by the trees, but his shadow defined itself clearly on the grass of the lawn. She could not distinguish the features of this person, but she was certain now that a man was lurking there. She watched him ten minutes, twenty minutes, half an hour. He did not move. It gave her such an eerie shock that it occurred to her that perhaps she was really going out of her mind. She closed her eyes and counted by sevens to two hundred and eighty. Then when she looked out again the shadow was gone.

Her husband knocked on the door. Receiving no answer, he turned the knob cautiously and peered inside. 'My dear, are you asleep?' he asked in a voice loud enough to wake anyone.

'Yes,' she said bitterly. 'Dead asleep.'

The Major, puzzled, did not know whether to shut the door or to come inside. All the way across the room she could sense the fact that he had made frequent visits to Leonora's sideboard.

'Tomorrow I am going to tell you something,' she said. 'You ought to have an inkling of what it's about. So prepare yourself.'

'I haven't any idea,' the Major said helplessly. 'Have I done something wrong?' He bethought himself for a few moments. 'But if it's money for anything peculiar, I don't have it, Alison. Lost a bet on a football game and board for my horse——' The door closed warily.

It was past midnight and she was alone again. These hours, from twelve o'clock until dawn, were always dreadful. If ever she told Morris that she had not slept at all, he, of course, did not believe her. Neither did he believe that she was ill. Four years ago, when her health first broke down, he had been alarmed by her condition. But when one calamity followed another—empyema, kidney trouble, and now this heart disease—he became exasperated and ended finally by not believing her. He thought it all a hypochondriacal fake that she used in order to shirk her duties—that is, the routine of sports and parties which he thought suitable. In the same way it is wise to give an insistent hostess a single, firm excuse, for if one declines with a number of reasons, no matter how sound they may be, the hostess will not believe you. She heard her husband walking about in his room across the hall and carrying on a long didactic conversation with himself. She switched on her bed light and began reading.

At two o'clock in the morning it came to her suddenly, without warning, that she was going to die that night. She sat propped up with pillows in the bed, a young woman with a face already sharp and aged, looking restlessly from one corner of the wall to another. She moved her head in a curious little gesture, lifting her chin upward and sideways, as though something were choking her. The silent room seemed to her full of jarring sounds. Water dripped into the bowl of the lavatory in the bathroom. The clock on the mantelpiece, an old pendulum clock with white and gilt swans painted on the glass of the case, ticked with a rusty sound. But the third of these sounds, the loudest and the one which bothered her most, was the beating of her own heart. A great turmoil was going on inside her. Her heart seemed to be vaulting—it would beat rapidly like the footsteps of someone running, leap up, and then thud with a violence that shocked her all over. With slow, cautious movements she opened the drawer of the bedside table and took out her knitting. 'I must think of something pleasant,' she told herself reasonably.

She thought back to the happiest time of her life. She was twenty-one and for nine months had been trying to work a little Cicero and Virgil into the heads of boarding-school girls. Then when vacation came she was in New York with two hundred dollars in her pocketbook. She had got on a bus and headed north with no idea where she was going. And somewhere in Vermont she came to a village she liked the looks of, got off, and within a few days found and rented a little shack out in the woods. She had brought her cat, Petronius, with her—and before the summer was over she was obliged to put a feminine ending onto his name because he suddenly had a litter of kittens. Several stray hounds took up with them and once a week she would go into the village to buy cans of groceries for the cats, the dogs, and herself. Morning and night, every day of that fine summer, she had her favorite foods—chili con carne, zwieback, and tea. In the afternoons she chopped firewood and at night she sat in the kitchen with her feet on the stove and read or sang aloud to herself.

Alison's pale, flaky lips shaped whispering words and she stared with concentration at the footboard of the bed. Then all at once she dropped the knitting and held her breath. Her heart had stopped beating. The room was silent as a sepulcher and she waited with her mouth open and her head twisted sideways on the pillow. She was terrified, but when she tried to call out and break this silence, no sound would come.

There was a light tapping on the door, but she did not hear this. Neither for a few moments did she realize that Anacleto had come into the room and was holding her hand in his. After the long, terrible silence (and surely it had lasted more than a minute), her heart was beating again; the folds of her nightgown fluttered lightly over her chest.

'A bad time?' Anacleto asked in a cheerful, encouraging little voice. But his face, as he looked down at her, wore the same sickly grimace as her own—with the upper lip drawn back sharply over the teeth.

'I was so frightened,' she said. 'Has something happened?'

'Nothing has happened. But don't look like that.' He took his handkerchief from the pocket of his blouse and dipped it in a glass of water to bathe her forehead. 'I'll go down and get my paraphernalia and stay with you until you can sleep.'

Along with his water-colors he brought a tray of malted milk. He built a fire and put up a card table before the hearth. His presence was such a comfort that she wanted to sob with relief. After he had given her the tray, he settled himself cozily at the table and drank his hot malted milk with slow, appreciative little sips. This was one of the things she loved the very most about Anacleto; he had a genius for making some sort of festival out of almost any occasion. He acted, not as though out of kindness he had left his bed in the dead of the night to sit up with a sick woman, but as though of their own free will they had chosen this particular hour for a very special party. Whenever they had anything disagreeable to go through with, he always managed to follow it up with some little treat. And now he sat with a white napkin over his crossed knees drinking the mixture with as much ceremony as if the cup had been filled with choice wine—although he disliked the taste of the stuff quite as much as she did, and only bought it because he was attracted by the glowing promises on the label of the can.

'Are you sleepy?' she asked.

'Not at all.' But at the very mention of sleep he was so tired that he could not keep from yawning. Loyally he turned away and tried to pretend that he had opened his mouth in order to feel one of his new wisdom teeth with his forefinger. 'I had a nap this afternoon and then I slept awhile tonight. I dreamed about Catherine.'

Alison could never think about her baby without experiencing an emotion so loaded with love and grief that it was like an insupportable weight on her chest. It was not true that time could muffle the keenness of this loss. Now she had more control over herself, but that was all. For a while, after those eleven months of joy, suspense, and suffering, she was quite unchanged. Catherine had been buried in the cemetery on the post where they were stationed. And for a long time she had been obsessed by the sharp, morbid image of the little body in the grave. Her horrified broodings on decay and on that tiny lonely skeleton had brought her to such a state that at last, after considerable red tape, she had had the coffin disinterred. She had taken what was left of the body to the crematorium in Chicago and had scattered the ashes in the snow. And now all that was left of Catherine were the memories that she and Anacleto shared together.

Alison waited until her voice should be steady and then she asked: 'What was it you dreamed?'

'It was troubling,' he said quietly. 'Rather like holding a butterfly in my hands. I was nursing her on my lap—then sudden convulsions—and you were trying to get the hot water to run.' Anacleto opened his paint box and arranged his paper, brushes, and water-colors before him. The fire brightened his pale face and put a glow in his dark eyes. 'Then the dream changed, and instead of Catherine I had on my knees one of the Major's boots that I had to clean twice today. The boot was full of squirming slithery new-born mice and I was trying to hold them in and keep them from crawling up all over me. Whoo! It was like——'

'Hush, Anacleto!' she said, with a shiver. 'Please!'

He began to paint and she watched him. He dipped his brush into the glass and a lavender

cloud showed in the water. His face was thoughtful as he bent over the paper and once he paused
to make a few rapid measurements with a ruler on
the table. As a painter Anacleto had great talent—of that she was sure. In his other accomplish-
ments he had a certain knack, but at bottom he
was imitative—almost, as Morris said, a little mon-
key. In his little water-colors, and drawings, however, he was quite himself. When they were stationed near New York, he had gone into the city in
the afternoons to the Art Students' League, and she
had been very proud, but not at all surprised, to
observe how many people at the school exhibition
came back to look at his pictures more than once.

His work was at once primitive and over-
sophisticated, and it laid a queer spell on the be-
holder. But she could not get him to take his gift
with proper seriousness and to work hard enough.

'The quality of dreams,' he was saying softly.
'That is a strange thing to think about. On afternoons in the Philippines, when the pillow is damp
and the sun shines in the room, the dream is of one
sort. And then in the North at night when it is
snowing——'

But already Alison had got back into her rut of
worry, and she was not listening to him. 'Tell me,'
she interrupted suddenly. 'When you had the sulks
this morning and said you were going to open a
linen shop in Quebec, did you have anything particular in mind?'

'Why, certainly,' he said. 'You know I have always wanted to see the city of Quebec. And I think there is nothing so pleasant as handling beautiful linen.'

'And that's all you had in mind——' she said. Her voice lacked the inflections of a question and he did not reply to this. 'How much money do you have in the bank?'

He thought a moment with his brush poised above the water glass. 'Four hundred dollars and six cents. Do you want me to draw it out?'

'Not now. But we might need it later.'

'For Heaven's sake,' he said, 'don't worry. It does not a particle of good.'

The room was filled with the rose glow of the fire and gray flickering shadows. The clock made a little whirring sound and then struck three.

'Look!' Anacleto said suddenly. He crumpled up the paper he had been painting on and threw it aside. Then he sat in a meditative gesture with his chin in his hands, staring at the embers of the fire. 'A peacock of a sort of ghastly green. With one immense golden eye. And in it these reflections of something tiny and——'

In his effort to find just the right word he held up his hand with the thumb and forefinger touched together. His hand made a great shadow on the wall behind him. 'Tiny and——'

'Grotesque,' she finished for him.

He nodded shortly. 'Exactly.'

But after he had already begun working, some sound in the silent room, or perhaps the memory of the last tone of her voice, made him turn suddenly around. 'Oh, don't!' he said. And as he rushed from the table he overturned the water glass so that it shattered on the hearth.

Private Williams had been in the room where the Captain's wife lay sleeping for only an hour that night. He waited near the outskirts of the woods during the party. Then, when most of the guests were gone, he watched through the sitting-room window until the Captain's wife went up-stairs to bed. Later he came into the house as he had done before. Again that night the moonlight was clear and silver in the room. The Lady lay on her side with her warm oval face cupped between her rather grubby hands. She wore a satin night-gown and the cover was pushed down to her waist. The young soldier crouched silent by the bedside. Once he reached out warily and felt the slippery cloth of her nightgown with his thumb and forefin-ger. He had looked about him on coming into the room. For a time he stood before the bureau and contemplated the bottles, powder-puffs, and toilet articles. One object, an atomizer, had aroused his interest, and he had taken it to the window and ex-amined it with a puzzled face. On the table there was a saucer holding a half-eaten chicken leg. The soldier touched it, smelled, and took a bite.

Now he squatted in the moonlight, his eyes half-closed and a wet smile on his lips. Once the Captain's wife turned in her sleep, sighed, and stretched herself. With curious fingers the soldier touched a brown strand of hair which lay loose on the pillow.

It was past three o'clock when Private Williams stiffened suddenly. He looked about him and seemed to listen to some sound. He did not realize all at once what caused this change, this uneasiness to come in him. Then he saw that the lights in the house next door had been turned on. In the still night he could hear the voice of a woman crying. Later he heard an automobile stop before the lighted house. Private Williams walked noiselessly into the dark hall. The door of the Captain's room was closed. Within a few moments he was walking slowly along the outskirts of the woods.

The soldier had slept very little during the past two days and nights and his eyes were swollen with fatigue. He made a half-circle around the post until he reached the shortest cut to the barracks. In this way he did not meet the sentry. Once in his cot he fell into a heavy sleep. But at dawn, for the first time in years, he had a dream and called out in his sleep. A soldier across the room awakened and threw a shoe at him.

As Private Williams had no friends among his barrack mates, his absence on these nights was of little interest to anyone. It was guessed that the

soldier had found himself a woman. Many of the
enlisted men were secretly married and sometimes
stayed the night in town with their wives. Lights
were out in the long crowded sleeping room at ten
o'clock, but not all of the men were in bed at this
hour. Sometimes, especially around the first of the
month, there were poker games in the latrine that
lasted the whole night through. Once at three
o'clock Private Williams had encountered the sentry on his way to the barracks, but as the soldier
had been in the army for two years and was familiar to the guard on duty, he was not questioned.

During the next few nights Private Williams
rested and slept normally. In the late afternoons he
sat alone on a bench before the barracks and at
night he sometimes frequented the places of
amusement on the post. He went to the movie and
to the gymnasium. In the evening the gymnasium
was converted into a roller-skating rink. There was
music and a corner set aside where the men could
rest at tables and drink cool, frothy beer. Private
Williams ordered a glass and for the first time
tasted alcohol. With a great rolling clatter the men
skated around in a circle and the air smelled
sharply of sweat and floor-wax. Three men, all
old-timers, were surprised when Private Williams
left his table to sit with them for a while. The
young soldier looked into their faces and seemed to
be on the point of asking some question of them.

But in the end he did not speak, and after a time he went away.

Private Williams always had been so unsociable that hardly half of his sleeping mates even knew his name. Actually the name he used in the army was not his own. On his enlistment a tough old Sergeant had glared down at his signature—L. G. Williams—and then bawled out at him: 'Write your name, you snotty little hayseed, your full name!' The soldier had waited a long time before revealing the fact that those initials were his name, and the only name he had. 'Well, you can't go into the U.S. Army with a goddam name like that,' the Sergeant said. 'I'll change it to E-l-l-g-e-e. O.K.?' Private Williams nodded and in the face of such indifference the Sergeant burst into a loud raw laugh. 'The half-wits they do send us now,' he had said as he turned back to his papers.

It was now November and for two days a high wind had blown. Overnight the young maples along the sidewalks were stripped of their leaves. The leaves lay in a bright gold blanket beneath the trees and the sky was filled with white changing clouds. The next day there was a cold rain. The leaves were left sodden and dun-colored, trampled on the wet streets, and finally raked away. The weather had cleared again and the bare branches of the trees made a sharp filigree against the winter sky. In the early morning there was frost on the dead grass.

After four nights of rest Private Williams returned to the Captain's house. This time, as he
knew the habits of the house, he did not wait until
the Captain had gone to bed. At midnight while
the officer worked in his study he went up to The
Lady's room and stayed an hour there. Then he
stood by the study window and watched curiously
until at two o'clock the Captain went upstairs. For
something was happening at this time that the soldier did not understand.

In these reconnoiterings, and during the dark
vigils in The Lady's room, the soldier had no fear.
He felt, but did not think; he experienced without
making any mental résumé of his present or past
actions. Five years before L. G. Williams had
killed a man. In an argument over a wheelbarrow
of manure he had stabbed a negro to death and
hidden the body in an abandoned quarry. He had
struck out in a fit of fury, and he could remember
the violent color of blood and the weight of the
limp body as he dragged it through the woods. He
could remember the hot sun of that July afternoon,
the smell of dust and death. He had felt a certain
wondering, numb distress, but there was no fear in
him, and not once since that time had the thought
shaped definitely in his mind that he was a mur-
derer. The mind is like a richly woven tapestry in
which the colors are distilled from the experiences
of the senses, and the design drawn from the con-
volutions of the intellect. The mind of Private Wil-

liams was imbued with various colors of strange tones, but it was without delineation, void of form.

Through these first winter days only one realization came to Private Williams, and it was this: he began to perceive that the Captain was following him. Twice a day, his face bandaged and still raw with rash, the Captain went out for short rides. And then when he had checked in the horse he lingered for a while before the stables. Three times on his way to mess Private Williams had looked behind him to see the Captain only about ten yards away. Far more often than chance could account for the officer passed him on the sidewalk. Once after one of these encounters the soldier stopped and looked behind him. After a short distance the Captain paused also and turned halfway around. It was late afternoon and the winter dusk had in it a pale violet tint. The Captain's eyes were steady, cruel, and bright. Almost a minute passed before, with one accord, they turned to continue on their ways.

iv

It is not easy on an army post for an officer to bring himself into personal contact with an enlisted man. Captain Penderton was now aware of this. Had he been serving as an ordinary line officer such as Major Morris Langdon, heading a company, a battalion, or a regiment, a certain amount of intercourse with the men in his command would have been open to him. Thus Major Langdon knew the name and face of almost every soldier in his charge. But Captain Penderton with his work at the School was in no such position. Except through his riding (and no feat of horsemanship was reckless enough for the Captain these days) there was no way at all for him to establish relations with the soldier whom he had come to hate.

Yet the Captain felt an aching want for contact between them of some sort. The thought of the soldier tantalized him continually. He went down to the stables as often as he could reasonably do so. Private Williams saddled his horse for him and held the bridle as he mounted. When the Captain knew in advance that he would meet the soldier, he felt himself grow dizzy. During their brief, impersonal meetings he suffered a curious lapse of sensory impressions; when he was near the soldier he found himself unable to see or to hear properly, and it was only after he had ridden away and was alone again that the scene developed itself for the first time in his mind. The thought of the young man's face—the dumb eyes, the heavy sensual lips that were often wet, the childish page-boy bangs—this image was intolerable to him. He rarely heard the soldier speak, but the sound of his slurring Southern voice meandered constantly in the back of his mind like a troubling song.

Late in the afternoons the Captain walked on the streets between the stables and the barracks in the hope of meeting Private Williams. When from a distance he saw him, walking with sluggish grace, the Captain felt his throat contract so that

he could scarcely swallow. Then, when they were
face to face, Private Williams always stared
vaguely over the Captain's shoulder and saluted
very slowly with his hand quite relaxed. Once as
they were nearing each other the Captain saw him
unwrap a bar of candy and drop the paper carelessly on the neat strip of grass bordering the sidewalk. This had infuriated the Captain and, after
walking for some distance, he turned back, picked
up the wrapper (it was from a bar of Baby Ruth),
and put it in his pocket.

Captain Penderton, who on the whole had lived
a most rigid and unemotional life, did not question
this strange hate of his. Once or twice, when he
awoke late after taking too much Seconal, he made
himself uncomfortable by thinking back over his
recent behavior. But he made no real effort to force
himself to an inward reckoning.

One afternoon he drove before the barracks and
saw the soldier resting alone on one of the benches.
The Captain parked his car farther down the street
and sat watching him. The soldier sprawled in the
abandoned position of one who is on the point of
napping. The sky was a pale green and the last of
the wintry sun made sharp, long shadows. The
Captain watched the soldier until the call for sup-
per. Then, when Private Williams had gone inside,
the Captain still sat in his car, looking at the outside of the barracks.

Dark came on and the building was brightly

lighted. In a recreation room downstairs he could
see the men playing billiards or lounging with mag-
azines. The Captain thought of the mess hall with
the long tables laden with hot food and the hungry
soldiers eating and laughing together with lusty camaraderie. The Captain was not familiar with enlisted men and his picture of the life inside the barracks was greatly enriched by his imagination. The
Captain was drawn toward the Middle Ages and
had made a careful study of European history during feudal times. His imaginings of the barracks
were flavored by this predilection. As he thought
of the two thousand men living together in this
great quadrangle, he felt suddenly alone. He sat in
the dark car and as he stared at the lighted,
crowded rooms inside, as he heard the sounds of
shouts and ringing voices, the tears came to his
glassy eyes. A bitter loneliness gnawed in him. He
drove quickly home.

Leonora Penderton was resting in the hammock
by the edge of the woods when her husband arrived. She went into the house and helped Susie
finish in the kitchen, as they were to dine at home
that evening and then go out to a party. A friend
had sent them half a dozen quail and she planned
to take over a tray to Alison, who had had a bad
heart attack on the night of their party more than
two weeks ago, and was now kept permanently in
bed. Leonora and Susie arranged the food on a
huge silver waiter. On a service plate they put two

quail and generous helpings of several vegetables, the juices of which ran together to form a little pool in the middle of the plate. There were a good many other dainties besides, and when Leonora staggered out carrying the big waiter, Susie had to follow after her with a tray holding the overflow.

'Why didn't you bring Morris home with you?' the Captain asked when she returned.

'Poor fellow!' said Leonora. 'He was already gone. Eating his meals at the Officers' Club. Think of it!'

They had dressed for the evening and were standing before the fire in the sitting-room with a bottle of whiskey and their glasses on the mantel-piece. Leonora wore her red crêpe frock and the Captain his tuxedo. The Captain was nervous and kept tinkling the ice in his glass.

'Hah! Listen!' he said suddenly. 'Here is a pretty good one I heard today.' He put his forefinger along the side of his nose and drew his lips back over his teeth. He was going to tell a story, and was sketching out the skeleton in advance. The Captain had a nice feeling for wit and was a sharp gossip.

'Not long ago there was a telephone call for the General, and the Adjutant, recognizing Alison's voice, put it through immediately. "General, here is a request," said the voice in a very poised and cul-tivated manner. "I want you to do me the great service of seeing to it that that soldier does not get up and blow his bugle at six o'clock in the morning. It disturbs Mrs. Langdon's rest." There was a long pause and at last the General said: "I beg your pardon, but I don't believe I quite understand you." The request was repeated, and there was a still longer pause. "And pray tell me," the General said finally, "whom do I have the honor of addressing?" The voice answered: "This is the *garçon de maison* to Mrs. Langdon, Anacleto. I thank you."'

The Captain waited soberly, for he was not one to laugh at his own jokes. Neither did Leonora laugh—she seemed puzzled.

'What did he say he was?' she asked.

'He was trying to say "houseboy" in French.'

'And you mean Anacleto called up like that about reveille. Well, if that doesn't beat anything I ever heard. I can hardly believe it!'

'Nit-wit!' said the Captain. 'It didn't really happen. It's just a story, a joke.'

Leonora did not get the point. She was no gossip. First, she always found it a little difficult to picture a situation that did not actually take place in the room with her. Also, she was not in the least malicious.

'Why, how mean!' she said. 'If it didn't happen, why should anyone go to the trouble to make it up? It makes Anacleto sound like a fool. Who do you suppose started it?'

The Captain shrugged and finished his drink. He had fabricated any number of ridiculous anecdotes about Alison and Anacleto, and they had all gone the rounds of the post with great success. The composition and sharpening of these scandalous vignettes afforded the Captain much pleasure. He launched them discreetly, making it understood that he was not the originator but was passing them on from some other source. He did this less out of modesty than from the fear that they might sometime come to the ears of Morris Langdon.

Tonight the Captain's new story did not please him. In the house alone with his wife he felt again the melancholy that had come to him while sitting out in the car before the lighted barracks. He saw in his mind the deft, brown hands of the soldier and felt himself shiver inwardly.

'What in the hell are you thinking about?' Leonora asked.

'Nothing.'

'Well, you look awfully peculiar to me.'

They had arranged to pick up Morris Langdon, and just as they were ready to leave he called for them to come over for a drink. Alison was resting, so they did not go upstairs. They had their drinks hurriedly at the dining-room table, as they were already late. When they were finished, Anacleto brought to the Major, who was in uniform, his military evening cape. The little Filipino followed them to the door and said very sweetly: 'I hope you have a pleasant evening.'

'Thank you,' said Leonora. 'Same to you.'

The Major, however, was not so guileless. He looked at Anacleto with suspicion.

When Anacleto had closed the door, he hurried into the sitting-room and drew back the curtain an inch to peek outside. The three of them, each of whom Anacleto hated with all his heart, had paused on the steps to light cigarettes. Anacleto watched with great impatience. While they had been in the kitchen a fine scheme had come to him. He had moved three bricks from the rose garden and placed them at the end of the dark front sidewalk. In his mind he saw all three of them tumbling like ninepins. When at last they strolled across the lawn toward the car parked before the Pendertons' house, Anacleto was so vexed that he gave his thumb a mean little bite. Then he hurried out to remove the obstruction, as he did not wish to catch anyone else in his snare.

The evening of that night was like any other evening. The Pendertons and Major Langdon went to a dance at the Polo Club and enjoyed themselves. Leonora had her usual rush from the young Lieutenants and Captain Penderton found the opportunity, over a quiet highball out on the veranda, to entrust his new story to a certain artillery officer who had a reputation as a wit. The Major stuck in the lounge with a cluster of his cronies, talking of fishing, politics, and ponies. There was to be a drag hunt the next morning and the Pendertons left with Major Langdon at about eleven o'clock. By

that hour Anacleto, who had stayed with his mis-
tress for a time and given her an injection, was in
bed. He always lay propped up with pillows, just
as did Madame Alison, although this position was
so uncomfortable that he could hardly ever get a
good night's rest. Alison, herself, was dozing. The
Major and Leonora were in their rooms and sleeping soundly by midnight. Captain Penderton had
settled down for a quiet period of work in his
study. It was a warm night for the month of November and the scent of the pines was balmy in
the air. There was no wind and shadows lay still
and dark on the lawns.

At about this time Alison Langdon felt herself
awaking from a half-sleep. She had had a series of
curious and vivid dreams that went back to the
time of her childhood, and she struggled against
returning consciousness. But such a struggle was
useless, and soon she was lying wide awake with
her eyes open to the dark. She began to cry, and
the sound of her soft nervous sobbing seemed not
to come from herself, but from some mysterious
sufferer out somewhere in the night. She had had a
very bad two weeks and she cried often. To begin
with, she was supposed to keep strictly to the bed,
as the doctor had told her that the next attack
would finish her. However, she had no high opinion of her doctor and privately she thought of him
as an old army saw-bones—and a first-class jackass
to boot. He drank, although he was a surgeon, and

once in an argument with her he had insisted that Mozambique was on the west instead of the east coast of Africa and would not admit his error until she got out an atlas; altogether she set little store by his opinions and advice. She was restless, and two days before she had suddenly felt such a longing to play the piano that she had got up, dressed, and gone downstairs when Anacleto and her husband were away. She played for a while and enjoyed herself. On the way back to her room she took the stairs very slowly and although she was very tired there were no ill effects.

The feeling of being trapped—because now she would certainly have to wait until she was better before going on with her plans—made her difficult to care for. At first they had had a hospital nurse, but the nurse and Anacleto did not get on well together and after a week she had left. Alison was continually imagining things. That afternoon a child somewhere in the neighborhood had screamed, as children often scream in play, and she had had the unreasonable fear that the child was hit by an automobile. She sent Anacleto rushing out into the street, and even after he had assured her that the children were only playing I-spy, she could not get over her anxiety. Then the day before she had smelled smoke and was certain the house was on fire. Anacleto went over every inch of the premises and still she was not reassured. Any sudden noise or trivial mishap would make her cry. Anacleto had bitten his fingernails to the quick and the Major stayed away from home as much as possible.

Now at midnight as she lay crying in the dark room another delusion came to her. She looked out of the window and saw again the shadow of a man on the Pendertons' back lawn. He was standing quite still, leaning against a pine tree. Then, as she watched him, he crossed the grass and went in by the back door. It came to her then with a fearful shock that this man, this skulker, was her own husband. He was sneaking in to Weldon Penderton's wife, even though Weldon himself was at home and working in his study. So great was her feeling of outrage that she did not stop to reason. Sick with anger she got out of bed and vomited in the bathroom. Then she put on a coat over her nightgown and stepped into a pair of shoes.

She did not hesitate on her way over to the Pendertons'. Nor did she once ask herself what she, who hated scenes above all things, would do in the situation which she was about to precipitate. She went in by the front way and closed the door behind her noisily. The hall was half-dark, as only a lamp was lighted in the sitting-room. Breathing painfully she climbed the stairs. Leonora's door was open and she saw the silhouette of a man squatting by the bedside. She stepped inside the room and switched on the lamp in the corner.

The soldier blinked in the light. He put his hand

to the window-sill and half-rose from his crouching position. Leonora stirred in her sleep, murmured, and turned over toward the wall. Alison stood in the doorway, her face white and twisted with amazement. Then without a word she backed out of the room.

In the meantime Captain Penderton had heard the front door open and close. He felt that something was amiss, but an instinct cautioned him to remain at his desk. He nibbled the eraser of his pencil and waited tensely. He had not known what to expect, but he was surprised when there was a knock on the door, and before he could reply Alison had come into the study.

'Why, whatever brings you here this time of the night?' the Captain asked with a nervous laugh.

She did not answer at once. She gathered the collar of her coat up close around her neck. When at last she spoke, her voice had a wooden tone, as if shock had deadened the vibrations. 'I think you had better go up to your wife's room,' she said.

This announcement, together with the strangeness of her appearance, startled the Captain greatly. But even stronger than his inward tumult was the thought that he must not lose his composure. In a flash a number of conflicting assumptions came to the Captain's mind. Her words could mean only one thing—that Morris Langdon was in Leonora's room. But surely not, for they would hardly be so willy-nilly as that! And if so what a position it would put him inl The Captain's smile was sugary and controlled. He did not reveal in any way his feelings of anger, doubt, and intense annoyance.

'Come, my dear,' he said in a motherly voice, 'you shouldn't be roaming around like this. I'll take you home.'

Alison gave the Captain a long piercing look. She seemed to be fitting together some mental puzzle. After a time she said slowly: 'You don't mean to sit there and tell me you know this and do nothing about it?'

Stubbornly the Captain retained his poise. 'I'll take you home,' he said. 'You're not yourself and you don't know what you're talking about.'

He got up hurriedly and took Alison by the arm. The feel of her frail, brittle elbow beneath the cloth of her coat repelled him. He hurried her down the steps and across the lawn. The front door of her house was open, but the Captain gave the doorbell a long ring. After a few moments Anacleto came into the hall, and before the Captain could make his departure he also saw Morris come out of his room at the top of the stairs. With mixed feelings of confusion and relief, he went back home, leaving Alison to explain herself as she chose.

The next morning Captain Penderton was not greatly surprised to learn that Alison Langdon had altogether lost her mind. By noon the whole post knew of this. (Her condition was referred to as a

'nervous breakdown,' but no one was misled by
this.) When the Captain and Leonora went over to
offer their services, they found the Major standing
outside the closed door of his wife's room, holding
a towel over his arm. He had been standing there
patiently almost all the day. His light-colored eyes
were wide with surprise and he kept twisting and
mashing the flap of his ear. When he came down
to see the Pendertons, he shook hands with them in
a strangely formal fashion and blushed painfully.

With the exception of the doctor, Major Langdon kept the details of this tragedy a secret in his
own shocked heart. Alison did not tear up the
sheets or foam at the mouth as he had imagined
the insane to do. On coming into the house in her
nightgown at one o'clock in the morning, she had
simply said that not only did Leonora deceive her
husband—but that she deceived the Major as well,
and with an enlisted man. Then Alison said that,
furthermore, she herself was going to get a divorce,
and she added that as she had no money she
would appreciate it if he, the Major, would lend
her the sum of five hundred dollars at four per cent
interest with Anacleto and Lieutenant Weincheck
as guarantors. In answer to his startled questions,
she said that she and Anacleto were going into
some business together or would buy a prawn
boat. Anacleto had hauled her trunk into the room
and all night he was busy packing under her super-
vision. They stopped off now and then to drink hot

tea and study a map to decide where they would go. Sometime before dawn they settled on Moultrieville, South Carolina.

Major Langdon was greatly shaken. He stood in the corner of Alison's room for a long time and watched them pack. He dared not open his mouth. After a long time, when all that she had said had soaked into his mind and he was forced to acknowledge to himself that she was crazy, he took her nail scissors and the fire tongs out of the room. Then he went downstairs and sat at the kitchen table with a bottle of whiskey. He cried and sucked the salty tears from his wet mustache. Not only did he grieve for Alison's sake, but he felt ashamed, as though this were a reflection on his own respectability. The more he drank the more his misfortune seemed to him incomprehensible. Once he rolled his eyes up toward the ceiling and called out in the silent kitchen with a questioning roar of supplication:

'God? O God—?'

Again he banged his head on the table until a knot came out on his forehead. By six-thirty in the morning he had finished more than a quart of whiskey. He took a shower, dressed, and telephoned Alison's doctor, who was a Colonel in the medical corps and the Major's own friend. Later another doctor was called in and they struck matches in front of Alison's nose and asked her various questions. It was during this examination that the Major had picked up the towel from the rack in her bathroom and put it over his arm. It gave him the look of being prepared for any emergency and was somehow a comfort to him. Before leaving, the Colonel talked for a long while, using the word 'psychology' many times, and the Major nodded dumbly at the end of every sentence. The doctor finished by advising that she be sent to a sanatorium as soon as possible.

'But look here,' the Major said helplessly. 'No strait-jacket or any place like that. You understand— where she can play the phonograph—comfortable. You know what I mean.'

Within two days a place in Virginia had been chosen. Due to hurry the institution had been selected more because of the price (it was astonishingly expensive) than for the therapeutic reputation. Alison only listened bitterly when the plans were told to her. Anacleto, of course, was going also. A few days later the three of them left on the train.

This establishment in Virginia catered to patients who were both physically and mentally ill. And the diseases that attack the body and the brain simultaneously are of a special kind. There were a number of old gentlemen who floundered about in a state of total confusion and had to keep a close watch on their unwieldy legs. There were a few lady morphinists and any number of rich young liquor-heads. But the place had a pretty terrace where tea was served in the afternoon, the gardens were well kept, and the rooms furnished luxuriously; the Major was satisfied and rather proud that he could afford it.

Alison, however, made no comment just at first. Indeed she did not speak at all to her husband until they sat down to dinner that night. As an exception, on the evening of her arrival she was to dine downstairs, but beginning with the next morning she was to rest in bed until the condition of her heart improved. At their table there were candles and hothouse roses. The service and the table linen were of the best quality.

Alison, however, seemed not to observe these niceties. On sitting down to the table she took in the room with one long, wandering gaze. Her eyes, dark and shrewd as always, examined the occupants at all the other tables. Then finally she spoke quietly and with bitter relish:

'My God, what a choice crew!'

Major Langdon was never to forget that dinner, for it was the last time he was with his wife. He left very early the next morning and stopped off to spend the night in Pinehurst where he had an old polo friend. Then, when he returned to the post a telegram was waiting for him. On the second night of her stay there Alison had had a heart attack and died.

This autumn Captain Penderton was thirty-five

years old. Despite his comparative youth he was soon to wear the maple leaves of a Major; and in the army, where promotion is largely contingent on seniority, this premature advancement was a marked tribute to his ability. The Captain had worked hard and his mind was brilliant from a military point of view—it was the opinion of many officers, including the Captain himself, that he would one day be a high ranking General. Nevertheless, Captain Penderton showed the strain of his long efforts. This autumn, especially during the past few weeks, he seemed to have aged disproportionately. There were bruise-like circles beneath his eyes and his complexion was of a yellow, mottled color. His teeth had begun to trouble him considerably. The dentist told him that two of the lower molars would have to be extracted and some bridgework put in, but the Captain kept deferring this operation, as he felt he did not have the time to spare. The Captain's face was habitually tense and a tic had developed in the muscles of his left eye. This spasmodic twitching of the eyelid gave to his drawn face a strangely paralyzed expression.

He was in a constant state of repressed agitation. His preoccupation with the soldier grew in him like a disease. As in cancer, when the cells unaccountably rebel and begin the insidious self-multiplication that will ultimately destroy the body, so in his mind did the thoughts of the soldier grow out of all proportion to their normal sphere.

Sometimes with dismay he made a wondering résumé of the steps that had brought about this condition—beginning with the carelessly spilt coffee on a new pair of trousers, and continuing with the clearing of the woods, the encounter after the ride on Firebird, and the brief meetings on the streets of the post. How his annoyance could have grown to hate, and the hate to this diseased obsession, the Captain could not logically understand.

A peculiar reverie had taken hold of him. As he always had been keenly ambitious, he had often amused himself by anticipating his promotions far in advance. Thus, when he was still a young West-Pointer the name and the title 'Colonel Weldon Penderton' had to him a familiar and pleasing sound. And during the past summer of this year he had imagined himself as a Corps Area Commander of great brilliance and power. Sometimes he had even whispered the words 'Major General Penderton' aloud to himself—and it seemed to him he should have been born to the title, so well did the sound of it fit with his name. But now during the past weeks this idle dream had strangely reversed itself. One night—or rather it was one-thirty in the morning—he had sat at his desk in a trauma of fatigue. Suddenly in the silent room three words had come unbidden to his tongue: 'Private Weldon Penderton.' And these words, with the associations they engendered, aroused in the Captain a perverse feeling of relief and satisfaction. Instead of dreaming of honor and rank, he now experienced a subtle pleasure in imagining himself as an enlisted man. In these phantasies he saw himself as a youth, a twin almost of the soldier whom he hated—with a young, easy body that even the cheap uniform of a common soldier could not make ungraceful, with thick glossy hair and round eyes unshadowed by study and strain. The image of Private Williams wove itself through all these day-dreams. And the background of all this was the barracks: the hubbub of young male voices, the genial loafing in the sun, the irresponsible shenanigans of camaraderie.

Captain Penderton had formed the habit of walking each afternoon before the quadrangle where Private Williams was quartered. Usually he saw the soldier sitting alone on the same bench. Walking on the sidewalk the Captain would pass within two yards of the soldier, and at his approach Private Williams would get up reluctantly and give a lazy salute. The days were growing short, and at this time in the late afternoon a hint of darkness was already in the air. For a brief period after sunset there was in the atmosphere a misty lavender glow.

The Captain on passing always looked full into the soldier's face and slowed his footsteps. He knew that the soldier must now realize that these afternoon walks were made on his account. It even occurred to the Captain to wonder why the soldier did not evade him and go elsewhere at this time. The fact that the soldier clung to his habit gave to these daily contacts a flavor of assignation that filled the Captain with excitement. After he had passed the soldier he had to suppress a craving to turn around, and as he walked away he felt his heart swell with a wild, nostalgic sadness which he could not control.

At the Captain's house there were a few changes. Major Langdon had attached himself to the Pendertons like a third member of the family, and this state of affairs was agreeable both to the Captain and Leonora. The Major was left quite stunned and helpless by the death of his wife. Even physically there was a difference in him. His jovial poise had deserted him, and when the three of them were sitting before the fire in the evening, he seemed to want to get himself into the most hobbledehoy and uncomfortable positions possible. He would twist his legs around each other like a contortionist or hike up one heavy shoulder while he mashed his ear. His thoughts and his words now centered entirely on Alison and the part of his life that had now come so abruptly to an end. He was inclined to make doleful platitudes concerning God, the soul, suffering, and death—subjects the mention of which would hitherto have made his tongue grow thick and awkward with embarrassment. Leonora looked after him, fed him excellent dinners, and listened to any mournful observations he might have to make.

'If only Anacleto would come back,' he said often.

For Anacleto had left the sanatorium the morning after Alison had died and no one had heard of him since. He had repacked the luggage and put all of her things in order. Then he had simply disappeared. To replace him Leonora had hired for the Major one of Susie's brothers who could cook. For years the Major had longed for an ordinary colored boy who would maybe steal his liquor and leave dust under the rug, but who at any rate, by God, would not fiddle around with the piano and jabber in French. Susie's brother was a good boy; he played on a comb wrapped in toilet paper, got drunk, and cooked good cornbread. But at the same time the Major did not feel the satisfaction he had anticipated. He missed Anacleto in many ways and felt concerning him the most uncomfortable remorse.

'You know I used to devil Anacleto by describing what I would do to him if I could get him into the service. You don't suppose the little rascal really believed me, do you? I was mostly kidding him—but in a way it always seemed to me that if he would enlist it would be the best thing in the world for him.'

The Captain was weary of the talk about Alison and Anacleto. It was a pity the nasty little Filipino

hadn't been carried off by a heart attack also. The
Captain was tired of almost everything around the
house these days. The plain, heavy Southern meals
that Leonora and Morris enjoyed were especially
distasteful to him. The kitchen was filthy and Susie
too slovenly for words. The Captain was a connois-
seur of good food and a neat amateur chef. He ap-
preciated the subtle cookery of New Orleans, and
the delicate, balanced harmony of French food.
Often in the old days he used to go into the
kitchen when he was in the house alone and prepare for his own enjoyment some luscious tidbit.
His favorite dish was fillet of beef à la Béarnaise.
However, the Captain was a perfectionist and a
crank; if the tournedos were too well done, or if
the sauce got hot and curdled even the slightest
bit—he would take it all out to the back yard, dig
a hole, and bury it. But now he had lost all appe-
tite for food. This afternoon Leonora had gone to
the movies and he sent Susie away. He had
thought that he would like to cook something special. But in the midst of preparing a rissole he had
suddenly lost all interest, left everything as it was,
and walked out of the house.

'I can imagine Anacleto on K.P.,' Leonora said.

'Alison always thought I brought up the subject
just to be cruel,' said the Major. 'But that wasn't so.
Anacleto wouldn't have been happy in the army,
no, but it might have made a man of him. Would

have knocked all the nonsense out of him anyway. But what I mean is that in a way it always seemed to me terrible for a grown man twenty-three years old to be dancing around to music and messing with water-colors. In the army they would have run him ragged and he would have been miserable, but even that seems to me better than the other.'

'You mean,' Captain Penderton said, 'that any fulfillment obtained at the expense of normalcy is wrong, and should not be allowed to bring happiness. In short, it is better, because it is morally honorable, for the square peg to keep scraping about the round hole rather than to discover and use the unorthodox square that would fit it?'

'Why, you put it exactly right,' the Major said. 'Don't you agree with me?'

'No,' said the Captain, after a short pause. With gruesome vividness the Captain suddenly looked into his soul and saw himself. For once he did not see himself as others saw him; there came to him a distorted doll-like image, mean of countenance and grotesque in form. The Captain dwelt on this vision without compassion. He accepted it with neither alteration nor excuse. 'I don't agree,' he repeated absently.

Major Langdon thought over this unexpected reply, but did not continue the conversation. He always found it difficult to follow up any one line of thought beyond the first, bare exposition. With a

headshake he returned to his own bewildering
affairs. 'Once I waked up just before daylight,' he
said. 'I saw the lamp was on in her room and I
went in. And there I found Anacleto sitting on the
edge of the bed and they were both of them looking down and fooling with something. And what
was it they were doing?' The Major pressed his
blunt fingers against his eyeballs and shook his
head again. 'Oh yes. They were dropping little
things into a bowl of water. Some sort of Japanese
mess Anacleto had bought at the ten-cent store—
these little particles open like flowers in the water.
And they were just sitting there at four o'clock in
the morning trifling with that. It made me suddenly irritable, and when I stumbled over Alison's
slippers by the side of the bed, I lost my temper
and kicked them across the room. Alison was disgusted with me, cold as ice for days. And Anacleto
put salt in the sugar bowl before he brought me
my coffee. It was sad. Those nights she must have
suffered.'

'They giveth it and then they taketh it away,'
said Leonora, whose intentions were better than
her command of Scripture.

Leonora herself had altered a little during the
past weeks. She was approaching the phase of her
full maturity. In this short time her body seemed to
have lost some of its youthful muscularity. Her
face was broader, and her expression in repose was
one of lazy tenderness. She looked like a woman

who has had several well-born babies and who hopefully expects another in about eight months. Her complexion was still of a delicate, healthy texture, and although she was gradually putting on weight there was as yet no sign of flabbiness. She had been dismayed by the death of her lover's wife. The sight of the dead body in the coffin had so fascinated her that for several days after the funeral she had spoken in an awed whisper, even when ordering groceries at the Post Exchange. She treated the Major with a sort of vacant sweetness and repeated any happy anecdotes concerning Alison that she could remember.

'By the way,' said the Captain suddenly, 'I can't stop wondering about that night—when she came over here. What did she say to you in your room, Leonora?'

'I told you I didn't even know she came. She didn't wake me up.'

But on this subject Captain Penderton was still unsatisfied. The more he remembered the scene in his study, the stranger and more compelling it became to him. He did not doubt that Leonora told the truth, for whenever she lied it was instantly plain to everyone. But what had Alison meant and why on coming back home had he not gone upstairs to see? He felt he knew the answer somewhere in the shadowy unconscious of his mind. But the more he thought about this matter, the sharper was his uneasiness.

'I remember one time when I was certainly surprised,' said Leonora, holding her pink, schoolgirlish hands out to the fire. 'It was when we all drove up to North Carolina, the afternoon after we ate those good partridges at the house of that friend of yours, Morris. Alison and Anacleto and I were walking along this country road when a little boy came along leading this plow horse—close kin to a mule, he was. But Alison liked the old plug's face and suddenly decided she wanted to ride him. So she made friends with the little Tarheel and then climbed up on a fence post and slipped on—no saddle and wearing a dress. Think of it! I guess the horse hadn't been ridden for years and soon as she got on him he just lay down and started to roll her. And I thought to myself that that was the end of Alison Langdon and shut my eyes. But do you know she had got that horse up in a minute and was trotting around the field as though nothing at all had happened. You never could have done it, Weldon. And Anacleto was running up and down like a drunk jay-bird. Lord, what a good time—I never was so surprised!'

Captain Penderton yawned, not because he was sleepy, but because Leonora's reference to his horsemanship had piqued him and he wanted to be discourteous. There had been some bitter scenes between the Captain and Leonora over Firebird. After the frenzied, runaway ride the horse had never been altogether the same, and Leonora blamed her husband vehemently. The events of the past two weeks, however, had served to deflect the course of their feud and the Captain was confident that soon she would forget.

Major Langdon closed this particular evening's conversation with one of his favorite aphorisms: 'Only two things matter to me now—to be a good animal and to serve my country. A healthy body and patriotism.'

At this time Captain Penderton's home was not an ideal place for a person undergoing an acute psychic crisis. Formerly the Captain would have found the laments of Morris Langdon ridiculous. But now there was the atmosphere of death in the house. To him it seemed that not only had Alison died, but that in some mysterious way the lives of all three of them had come to a close. The old fear that Leonora might divorce him and go away with Morris Langdon did not trouble him any more. Any inclination he had once had toward the Major seemed now a mere velleity compared to his feelings for the soldier.

The house itself irritated the Captain exceedingly these days. Their quarters were furnished in haphazard fashion. In the sitting-room there was the conventional sofa covered with flower-patterned chintz, a couple of easy-chairs, a rug of garish red, and an antique secretary. The room had an air of flossiness that the Captain abhorred. The lace curtains looked cheap and rather dingy, and on the mantelpiece there was a heterogeneous collection of ornaments and gewgaws—a procession of sham-ivory elephants, a pair of beautiful wrought-iron candlesticks, a painted statuette of a pickaninny grinning over a red slice of watermelon, and a blue glass Mexican bowl into which Leonora had dumped old visiting cards. All of the furniture was slightly rickety from too much moving, and the feminine, cluttered impression made by the room as a whole so exasperated the Captain that he stayed out of it as much as possible. With deep secret longing he thought of the barracks, seeing in his mind the neat cots placed in a row, the bare floors, and stark curtainless windows. Against one of the walls of this imaginary room, ascetic and austere, there was for some reason an ancient carved chest with brass bindings.

Captain Penderton on his long walks during the late afternoon was in a state of sharpened sensitivity close to delirium. He felt himself adrift, cut off from all human influence, and he carried with him the brooding image of the young soldier much as a witch would hug to her bosom some cunning charm. He experienced during this time a peculiar vulnerability. Although he felt himself isolated from all other persons, the things which he saw on his walks took on an abnormal importance in his eyes. Everything with which he came in contact, even the most commonplace objects, seemed to have some mysterious bearing on his own destiny.

If, for instance, he chanced to notice a sparrow in the gutter, he could stand for whole minutes, completely absorbed in this ordinary sight. For the time being he had lost the primitive faculty that instinctively classifies the various sensory impressions according to their relative values. One afternoon he saw a transport truck run into an automobile. But this bloody accident impressed him no more vividly than the sight, a few minutes later, of a scrap of newspaper fluttering in the wind.

For a long time now he had ceased to attribute his feelings for Private Williams to hate. Also he no longer tried to find justification for the emotion that had so taken possession of him. He thought of the soldier in terms neither of love nor hate; he was conscious only of the irresistible yearning to break down the barrier between them. When from a distance he saw the soldier resting before the barracks, he wanted to shout to him, or to strike him with his fist, to make him respond in some way to violence. It was almost two years now since he had first seen the soldier. More than a month had gone by since he had been sent on special fatigue to clear the woods. And in all this time they had hardly spoken to each other more than a few dozen words.

On the afternoon of the twelfth of November, Captain Penderton went out as usual. He had had a trying day. That morning in the classroom, while standing before the blackboard in the process of illustrating a tactical problem, he had had an unexplainable attack of amnesia. In the middle of a sentence his mind went blank. Not only did he totally forget every word of the remainder of his lecture, even the faces of the student officers in the room seemed unfamiliar to him. In his mind he could see Private Williams very clearly—that was all. For some moments he stood dumbly with the chalk still in his hand. Then he found presence of mind to dismiss the class. Fortunately the lecture was almost ended when his lapse had occurred.

The Captain walked very stiffly along one of the sidewalks leading toward the quadrangle. The weather on this afternoon was extraordinary. There were dour storm clouds in the sky, but down near the horizon the heavens were still clear and the sun shone with gentle radiance. The Captain swung his arms as though they would not bend at the elbow and kept his eyes on the bottoms of his army slacks and his highly polished narrow shoes. He looked up just as he reached the bench where Private Williams sat, and after staring at him for a few seconds he went up to him. Sluggishly the soldier rose to attention.

'Private Williams,' the Captain said.

The soldier waited, but Captain Penderton did not continue. He had meant to reprimand the soldier for a violation of the regulations concerning the uniform. As he approached, it had seemed to him that Private Williams had buttoned his coat improperly. At first glance the soldier always looked as though he were only in partial uniform, or had neglected some necessary part of his attire. But when they were face to face, Captain Penderton saw that there was nothing for him to criticize. The impression of civilian carelessness was due to the very body of the soldier himself and to no particular infringement of army rules. Again the Captain stood mute and suffocated before the young man. In his heart there coursed a wild tirade of curses, words of love, supplications, and abuse. But in the end he turned away, still silent.

The rain that had been threatening held off until Captain Penderton was almost home. This was not a slow, drizzling winter rain—it came down with the roaring vehemence of a summer thunderstorm. The Captain was within twenty yards of his house when the first drops fell on him. With a short sprint he could have easily reached shelter. But his dragging footsteps did not quicken, even when the icy, pouring torrent soaked into him. When he opened his front door he was bright-eyed and shivering.

Private Williams went into the barracks when he scented in the atmosphere the coming rain. He sat in the day-room until supper-time and then, amid the rowdy exuberance of the mess hall, he ate a copious, leisurely meal. Afterward he took from his locker a sack of mixed penny candies.

While still chewing a marshmallow, he paid a visit to the latrine and there he picked a fight. At the time of his entrance all of the commodes except one were in use, and there was a soldier ahead of him in the act of unbuttoning his trousers. But just as the man started to sit down, Private Williams gave him a rough push and tried to oust him from his place. A little crowd gathered about the fight which followed. From the first Private Williams had the best of it, as he was both quick and strong. While fighting, his face expressed neither effort nor anger; his features still were impassive and only the sweat on his forehead, the look of blindness in his eyes, showed the results of his struggle. Private Williams had his opponent in a helpless condition and the fight was already won when all at once he himself suddenly gave up. He seemed completely to lose interest in the fight and did not even bother to defend himself. He was soundly beaten and his head was banged viciously against the cement floor. When it was over, he stood up groggily and left the latrine without even using the commode after all.

This was not the first fight that Private Williams had provoked. During the past two weeks he had stayed in the barracks every night, and had stirred up much trouble. This was a new side of his personality that his barrack mates had not suspected. For hours he would sit in torpid silence and then all at once he would perpetrate some inexcusable offense. He no longer walked in the woods in his spare time, and at night he slept badly, disturbing the room with nightmare mutters. No one, however, gave any thought to his oddities. There was much behavior in the barracks far queerer than this. One old Corporal wrote a letter every night to Shirley Temple making it a sort of diary of all that he had done during the day, and mailing it before breakfast the next morning. Another man, who had ten years' service behind him, jumped out of a three-story window because a friend would not lend him fifty cents for beer. A cook in the same battery was haunted by the fixed idea that he had cancer of the tongue, an illusion that no medical denials could dispel. He brooded before a mirror with his tongue out so far that he could see the taste-buds, and he starved himself to the point of emaciation.

After the fight Private Williams went to the sleeping room and lay down on his cot. He put the sack of candy beneath his pillow and stared up at the ceiling. Outside the rain had slackened and it was now night. A number of lazy reveries colored the mind of Private Williams. He thought of the Captain, but he only saw a series of mental pictures that had no meaning. To this young Southern soldier the officers were in the same vague category as Negroes—they had a place in his life, but he did not look on them as being human. He accepted the Captain as fatalistically as though he

were the weather or some natural phenomenon.
The Captain's behavior might seem unexpected,
but he did not identify it with himself. And it did
not occur to him to question it, any more than he
would question a thunderstorm or the fading of a
flower.

He had not been near the quarters of Captain
Penderton since the night the lamp had been
switched on and he saw the dark woman looking at
him from the doorway. At that time a great fright
had come in him—but this terror had been more
physical than mental, more unconscious than understood. After he had heard the front door shut,
he had looked out cautiously and seen the way
clear. Once safe again in the woods he had run
desperately, silently, although he did not realize
exactly what it was he feared.

But the memory of the Captain's wife had not
left him. He dreamed of The Lady every night.
Once, soon after his enlistment, he had got pto-
maine poisoning and had been sent into hospital.
The thought of the bad sickness in women had
made him shudder beneath the cover whenever the
nurses came near him, and he had lain for hours in
misery rather than ask of them some service. But
he had touched The Lady and he was afraid of this
sickness no more. Every day he groomed and saddled her horse and watched her ride away. In the
early morning there was a wintry bitterness in the
air and the Captain's wife was rosy and high-

spirited. She always had a joke or a friendly word for Private Williams, but he never looked at her directly or answered her pleasantries.

He never thought of her in connection with the stables or the open air. To him she was always in the room where he had watched her in the night with such absorption. His memory of these times was wholly sensual. There was the thick rug beneath his feet, the silk spread, the faint scent of perfume. There was the soft luxurious warmth of woman-flesh, the quiet darkness—the alien sweetness in his heart and the tense power in his body as he crouched there near to her. Once having known this he could not let it go; in him was engendered a dark, drugged craving as certain of fulfillment as death.

The rain stopped at midnight. Long ago the lights in the barracks had been turned off. Private Williams had not undressed himself, and when the rain was over he put on his tennis shoes and went outside. On his way to the Captain's quarters he took his usual route, skirting the woods surrounding the post. But tonight there was no moon and the soldier was walking much faster than usual. Once he lost himself, and when at last he reached the Captain's house he had an accident. In the darkness he stumbled into what seemed to him at first to be a deep pit. In order to get his bearings he struck a few matches and saw that he had fallen into a recently dug hole. The house was dark, and the soldier, who was now scratched, muddy, and breathless, waited a few moments before going inside. In all he had come six times before, and this was the seventh and would be the last.

Captain Penderton was standing at the back window of his bedroom. He had taken three capsules, but still he could not sleep. He was slightly drunk with brandy, and a little drugged—but that was all. The Captain, who was keenly sensitive to luxury and a finicky dresser, wore only the coarsest sleeping garments. He had on now a wrapper of rough black wool that might have been bought for a recently widowed matron of a jail. His pajamas were of some unbleached material as stiff as canvas. He was barefooted, although the floor was now cold.

The Captain was listening to the sough of the wind in the pine trees when he saw out in the night a tiny flicker of flame. The light was blown out by the wind in only a moment, but during that instant the Captain had seen a face. And that face, brightened by the flame and set in darkness, made the Captain stop his breath. He watched and could vaguely make out the figure that crossed the lawn. The Captain clutched the front of his wrapper and pressed his hand against his breast. He closed his eyes and waited.

At first no sound came to him. Then he could feel rather than hear the cautious footsteps on the stairs. The Captain's door was ajar and through the crack he saw a dark silhouette. He whispered something, but his voice was so sibilant and low that it sounded like the wind outside.

Captain Penderton waited. With his eyes closed again, he stood there for moments of anguished suspense. Then he went out into the hall and saw outlined against the pale gray window of his wife's room the one for whom he sought. Afterward the Captain was to tell himself that in this one instant he knew everything. Actually, in a moment when a great but unknown shock is expected, the mind instinctively prepares itself by abandoning momentarily the faculty of surprise. In that vulnerable instant a kaleidoscope of half-guessed possibilities project themselves, and when the disaster has defined itself there is the feeling of having understood beforehand in some supernatural way. The Captain took his pistol from the drawer of his bed-table, crossed the hall, and switched on the light in his wife's room. As he did this, certain dormant fragments of memory—a shadow at the window, a sound in the night—came to him. He said to himself that he knew all. But what it was he knew he could not have expressed. He was only certain that this was the end.

The soldier did not have time to rise from his squatting position. He blinked at the light and there was no fear in his face; his expression was one of dazed annoyance, as if he had been inexcusably disturbed. The Captain was a good marksman, and although he shot twice only one raw hole was left in the center of the soldier's chest.

The reports from the pistol aroused Leonora and she sat up in bed. As yet she was still only half-awake, and she stared about her as though witnessing some scene in a play, some tragedy that was gruesome but not necessary to believe. Almost immediately Major Langdon knocked on the back door and then hurried up the stairs wearing slippers and a dressing-gown. The Captain had slumped against the wall. In his queer, coarse wrapper he resembled a broken and dissipated monk. Even in death the body of the soldier still had the look of warm, animal comfort. His grave face was unchanged, and his sun-browned hands lay palms upward on the carpet as though in sleep.

ABOUT THE AUTHOR

When she was only twenty-three, CARSON McCULLERS' first novel, *The Heart Is a Lonely Hunter*, became a literary sensation. Since that time Mrs. McCullers has written *Reflections in a Golden Eye*, *The Member of the Wedding*, *The Ballad of the Sad Café* and *Clock Without Hands*. Edward Albee's dramatization of *The Ballad of the Sad Café* appeared on Broadway. *The Member of the Wedding* was a prize-winning Broadway play and a motion picture.

Mrs. McCullers has steadily acquired an international reputation, with French and English critics ranking her close to Faulkner and Hemingway. *Time* placed her "among the top dozen contemporary American writers." She died in 1967.